"I'm worried that what you're doing is heedless."

"Maybe I don't care," Julia said. "Maybe I want to be reckless. Maybe I'm sick of following all the rules. I always obeyed orders like a good soldier and look where it got me." She held up her scarred hand. "Even if the nightmares end, I'll live with what Darcy did to me forever. It's not wrong to want her held responsible for what she did to me—and others."

"I'm not saying she shouldn't..." Martinez began.

"But I guess if I'm going to be reckless in one way, I should be reckless in all ways."

She traced the toe of her shoe up his calf.

He wasn't a stupid man. Martinez knew there was more than a little bit of innuendo to what Julia was saying and doing. He met her stare and his pulse began to race.

"Don't offer yourself to me unless you're serious," he said.

"Like I said, I'm tired of being so damned serious. Maybe I want to take a risk or two."

"Am I a risk you want to take?" he asked.

* * *

Dear Reader,

In *Agent's Wyoming Mission*, you'll meet one of my all-time favorite couples, Luis Martinez and Julia McCloud. Both Luis and Julia made their first appearance in *Rocky Mountain Valor*, the third book in my previous Rocky Mountain Justice miniseries.

Luis was a police officer with enough secrets to ruin his career. Julia, the only woman on a team of men, has always been able to hold her own.

As soon as I completed writing *Rocky Mountain Valor*, I knew one thing: Julia and Luis needed a story of their own. It was obvious to me that they were perfect for one another. It was also obvious to me that neither of them wanted to admit how much they cared.

Through three books, Luis has been a good teammate and a better friend. But he has a past—mistakes made and lives lost. That past is always under the surface and pushing him to do better and be better.

Julia's life has been gilded from the beginning. But she has wounds—both physical and emotional—of her own.

In *Agent's Wyoming Mission*, they both have to face everything that haunts them, all while searching for a new and devious killer. Can they do it all while being drawn to one another?

I hope you enjoy reading *Agent's Wyoming Mission* as much as I enjoyed writing it! Because one thing I do know—everyone deserves a happily-ever-after.

Regards,

Jennifer D. Bokal

AGENT'S WYOMING MISSION

Jennifer D. Bokal

Recycling programs for this product may not exist in your area.

ISBN-13: 978-1-335-62891-6

Agent's Wyoming Mission

This edition published by arrangement with Harlequin Books S.A.

For questions and comments about the quality of this book, please contact us at CustomerService@Harlequin.com.

Harlequin Enterprises ULC
22 Adelaide St. West, 40th Floor
Toronto, Ontario M5H 4E3, Canada
www.Harlequin.com

Printed in U.S.A.

Jennifer D. Bokal penned her first book at age eight. An early lover of the written word, she decided to follow her passion and become a full-time writer. From then on, she didn't look back. She earned a master of arts in creative writing from Wilkes University and became a member of Romance Writers of America and International Thriller Writers.

She has authored several short stories, novellas and poems. Winner of the Sexy Scribbler in 2015, Jennifer is also the author of the ancient-world historical series the Champions of Rome and the Harlequin Romantic Suspense series Rocky Mountain Justice.

Happily married to her own alpha male for more than twenty years, she enjoys writing stories that explore the wonders of love. Jen and her manly husband live in upstate New York with their three beautiful daughters, two very spoiled dogs and a kitten that aspires to one day become a Chihuahua.

Books by Jennifer D. Bokal

Harlequin Romantic Suspense

Wyoming Nights

Under the Agent's Protection
Agent's Mountain Rescue
Agent's Wyoming Mission

Rocky Mountain Justice

Her Rocky Mountain Hero
Her Rocky Mountain Defender
Rocky Mountain Valor

Visit the Author Profile page at Harlequin.com for more titles.

To John,
my forever happily-ever-after

Prologue

From the Pleasant Pines Gazette
August 12th edition

Big news for Pleasant Pines! Town-council spokesperson Everly Baker released a statement today naming Julia McCloud as the new sheriff, replacing Carl Haak. Given the emergency circumstances, McCloud was appointed for a one-year term.

Haak served in the position for over three decades before his death in March of this year. He was set to retire at the end of the month, but was murdered by serial killer Darcy Owens in an event that shocked the community. "We will continue to seek justice," said Baker.

McCloud, a graduate of the United States Military Academy at West Point, was an army ranger and served two tours overseas, one in Afghanistan and one in Iraq. After a decade in the military, she retired with the rank of captain. Her résumé also lists a tenure in private security.

In the statement, McCloud says, "I am happy to be serving the community of Pleasant Pines. My main priority is to discover the identity of whoever helped Darcy Owens get hired at the White Winds Resort in April." That individual could be complicit in the demise of McCloud's predecessor, Sheriff Haak.

Sheriff McCloud can be reached at the sheriff's office. She will also be attending the town council meeting at the end of the month with a welcome reception to follow. Refreshments provided by Sally's on Main. If you plan to attend, contact Everly Baker.

When asked if she would do anything differently, Sheriff McCloud spoke again about her predecessor. "Carl Haak was a good man. During my one-year term, I will work hard every day to provide Pleasant Pines with the same dedication he did. No matter what."

Chapter 1

Two months later

Julia McCloud held the gun with her left hand. Her heartbeat thundered, her pulse echoing in her ears. Lining up the sight, she pulled the trigger. Two quick pops. The silhouette remained untouched as dust exploded from the ground.

She cursed in frustration.

It was mid-October, one of the last pleasant weekends of the year. The distant hills were awash in all the colors of autumn—vibrant yellow, bright orange and deep burgundy. Yet she didn't care about the changing seasons—what she wanted was better aim.

Sweat dampened her hairline, despite the fact that she had pulled her locks into a high ponytail. The fabric of her white T-shirt clung to her back and dust coated her aviator sunglasses.

Julia, the newly appointed sheriff of Pleasant Pines, Wyoming, had three things on her mind. First was finding the unknown accomplice of Darcy Owens. Several months ago, Darcy had evaded capture by posing as an employee at the White Winds, a posh resort several hours from Pleasant Pines. Before her identity was discovered, she'd committed several murders in Pleasant Pines, placing the case in Julia's jurisdiction. The killer had been captured and jailed, and was currently awaiting trial. But the question of who'd gotten her the job in the first place was one that kept Julia awake at night.

Second was the ongoing search for Christopher Booth, the missing leader of the Transgressors, a motorcycle club. For years, Booth produced and sold drugs in Pleasant Pines. He was also wanted for kidnapping and human trafficking. Booth had escaped a raid—organized by the sheriff's office where she now worked and Rocky Mountain Justice, her former employer—and remained at large. Julia felt his continued freedom was a stain on her record.

The final, and most pressing, problem was Julia's inability to hit the damn target with her left hand.

The firing range sat on several arid acres outside of town. In all honesty, Julia was shocked that the private gun club was vacant on a sunny Saturday afternoon. She was relieved, all the same. At least there was nobody around to witness her failure.

The sheriff's failure.

Julia rolled her shoulders, then took aim again and fired twice, missing again both times. She tried to tell herself that it was okay. Except, nothing had been okay—not for a long time.

Several months earlier, the Darcy Owens case had changed her life forever. Before she'd become sheriff, Julia and her team had discovered a big break—a bunker ideal for a murderer on the run. But Julia had been caught by the murderer and attacked. During that violent confrontation, she had lost two fingers, and had also taken an ax blade to the stomach.

Sure, she was happy to be alive. Thanks to her colleagues at Rocky Mountain Justice, or RMJ. All the same, what she really wanted was to live again. To do the things that made her independent—like hitting a damn target that was a mere twenty-five yards away. Something that had been second nature.

Before.

With a deep breath, Julia cleared her mind. Like she'd been taught at Ranger School, Julia visualized the bullet punching a neat hole through the wooden silhouette. She saw it. She believed it. She knew it was possible.

Lifting her gaze, Julia stared at the black outline of a head and torso surrounded by blinding white. She pulled the trigger once. Twice. Her aim was still off, and she hit nothing. Arm outstretched, she stepped forward, bringing her toes even with the firing line. In the army, she had earned marksman status.

But the target remained unblemished.

Ignoring the safety rules, Julia stepped out into

her lane, moving in closer and closer. Dust filled the air as bullets struck the ground.

Standing a foot from the target, Julia lifted her arm and pressed the barrel of her gun into the wooden board…right in the middle of the forehead. She pulled the trigger once more. *Click.* The magazine was empty.

"What the hell are you doing?"

Luis Martinez, at the end of his lane, called out to Julia. He was standing in a wooden stall, and overhead a tin roof glinted with sunlight. He was wearing a pair of snug-fitting jeans and a Colorado Mustangs T-shirt. Lowering his own gun, he stared at her. "You can't walk onto the firing range. What if you'd gotten shot?"

After sliding her gun into the holster at her hip, Julia started walking toward Luis. "There's nobody around. Sure, I broke a few rules, but what of it? You aren't going to accidentally shoot me."

"When you asked me to come with you to the firing range, I didn't think you'd be reckless enough to expose yourself to live fire." Luis's dark eyes were filled with fury and something else she couldn't name.

Concern?

A momentary pang of guilt gripped her chest. She didn't want Luis—or anyone, really—to worry about her. Yet, what could she say about her behavior? How could she explain what she'd done, when Julia wasn't sure she actually understood?

For a long moment, they stared at each other. Luis

worked his jaw back and forth. Finally, he spoke. "I think we're done here."

"Probably," she said. How could she put into words that she felt as if she'd lost all control? It wasn't just the attack, where she'd clearly been the victim. But Julia still hadn't reclaimed her life. Despite months of physical and occupational therapy, she was no better off than when she'd left the hospital in Cheyenne.

And forget about the nightmares...

Luis had been with her through it all. More than being her partner when she was at RMJ, he was a good friend. She could confide in him. "Every time I go to sleep it's the same nightmare. Me. Darcy. The bunker. What she did to me." She hesitated. "The way I failed."

Luis's bronze complexion paled. "This has been so hard on you. But I didn't know you weren't sleeping, either."

"Even during the day, I can't shake the memories of what happened. That's why I wanted to get out of the house, you know. Today's been a disaster." Glancing at her right hand, Julia's mouth went dry. The fingerless sockets, the red scarred flesh. Yet, the ghosts of the two fingers she'd lost still tingled with remembered feeling. Maybe someday she'd be whole again. It'd mean more surgeries, maybe prosthetics. First, she had more healing to do. But where did that leave her now? "If I can't shoot, I can't work. It means that despite the fact that Darcy is in jail, she won."

"You're still healing. You have to relearn some things—like how to fire a gun."

"Relearn?" Julia snorted. "I didn't hit the target once. I was never this bad, even the first time my dad showed me how to use his revolver when I was a kid."

Placing a hand on her shoulder, he said, "Things will get better. Maybe I can help you work on your grip. I did teach at the police academy in Denver, you know."

His touch was soothing. Looking at him now, she couldn't help but notice his shoulders were broad, his arms strong. Certainly, he could help bear Julia's burdens. All she had to do was lean in to his embrace... But she wasn't in the mood to be soothed.

"Don't," she said, moving away. "I don't want your sympathy. Or your help."

"I don't feel sorry for you," said Luis. "You're the toughest person I know. I watched you fight for your life. You won that battle, Julia. From now on, everything else is simple. And as far as help...man. Everyone needs help now and again—even you." Sighing, he continued, "I can help you, if you let me."

Her throat burned. Julia looked away. "Darcy took away my ability to protect myself...or protect others. If I can't do my job, if I can't work...then I've lost my purpose."

"You work hard at physical therapy. Occupational therapy. Things will get better." He paused. "You'll get better."

"What if I don't? I can't be the sheriff if I can't

hit the broad side of a barn. What would I do with myself, career-wise?"

He said, "All of us working cases in Pleasant Pines, the sheriff's office and RMJ—we're all a family."

"It's not, Luis," she said. "It's a job. And if I can't pull my weight, they'll kick me out."

Her voice caught on the last word, the only sign that she had lied to her friend. For her, protecting the community and enforcing the law was more than employment. It was a calling.

"You look miserable," he said.

"I feel worse." Julia tried to smile at her feeble joke.

"What can I do?" Luis asked. "How can I help?"

Help. There was that word again. She wanted to surrender to the solace he offered. Yet, wanting help and comfort made her weak. She loathed the idea of needing another person for emotional support. She was more of a lone wolf, able to sustain herself.

"I should go," she said, slipping away.

She didn't wait to see what else Luis would say. Julia stalked to her car and flung open the door. After stowing her gun in the glovebox, she slid behind the steering wheel. She turned the key in the ignition, slammed the gearshift into Drive and dropped her foot on the accelerator. As she drove, her tires kicked up a cloud of khaki-colored dust, erasing whatever past Julia was leaving behind.

She hit the contact app on her phone, placing a

call before she realized what she'd done. The phone was answered on the third ring by voice mail.

"This is Cheryl McCloud." Julia's mom used her most chipper voice for the outgoing message. "I can't get your call right now, so leave me a message and I'll get back to you soon."

The pang of panic—the one that had compelled her to call her mother—was barely a twinge. But she couldn't just hang up. Her mother would see her number on caller ID and worry. Clearing her throat, Julia put a smile into her voice. "Hi, Mom. It's me. Just seeing what you're up to. Call back whenever. Love you. Bye."

Using controls on the steering wheel, she ended the call. In the silence, Luis's words echoed in Julia's head. *I can help you, if you let me.*

Julia glanced in the rearview mirror. Hand shading his eyes, Luis stood in the middle of the parking lot and watched her drive away.

She was sure he could help her…and really, that was part of the problem. Julia didn't want to rely on anyone, even someone she respected, like Luis Martinez.

Luis Martinez watched as Julia's car disappeared from view. As the bumper faded to nothing, his chest tightened until he couldn't draw a full breath. It was the same feeling he'd had back in the day when he'd played football and gotten knocked on his ass.

This was no game and he wasn't a kid anymore.

What the hell had he done to piss off Julia? With

a shake of his head, he pulled his phone from his pocket and sent a text to his fellow agent and friend Liam Alexander. Meet me for a beer. Pleasant Pines Inn.

Liam answered immediately. In the middle of the afternoon?

True, Liam had a three-year-old daughter, Sophie. He might not be available to drop everything. Luis typed his response. I have problems. But don't worry. If you're busy, I can handle it on my own.

Liam's response: On my way.

The trip from the firing range to the Pleasant Pines Inn took less than twenty minutes. Liam's silver car was already in the parking lot as he arrived. He pulled into the next space and killed the engine. Striding through the lobby, he turned left and entered the pub. A long mahogany bar stood along one wall. Several tables filled the rest of the space and a parquet dance floor sat in the middle of the room.

For a split second, Luis recalled photographing every inch of this space. It had been months ago when they'd found the body of Larry Walker, the inn's cook, hanging in the kitchen. At the time, the evidence pointed to Larry killing himself after being identified as a serial killer. In the end, Darcy Owens had been the culprit.

He blinked, clearing the memories. At this time of the afternoon, on a Saturday, the bar was all but empty. One table was filled with a group of guys in expensive mountain-biking gear—obviously guests at the inn. A few locals—men and women both—in flannel shirts and jeans sat along the expanse of the bar and stared at a baseball game on a flat-screen TV. It was the playoffs—the team from Denver versus one of the teams from New York.

At the end of the bar, Liam Alexander was sitting on a stool. Liam wore a button-up canvas shirt, untucked. His dark hair skimmed the collar of his shirt. He raised a bottle of beer as Luis entered the room.

The bartender looked up as he slid onto the stool next to Liam's. "What can I get for you?"

"I'll have what he's drinking." The bartender slid a bottle toward Martinez. "Thanks."

Lifting the beer to his lips, he took a sip. "Women," he muttered.

"All women?" Liam asked. "Or is there one in particular?"

"Just one. I can't handle any more."

"I have Holly and Sophie, and they keep me busy." Liam gave an exaggerated eye roll. "They were painting their toenails when I left. If you hadn't texted when you did, I might be getting a pedicure right now."

The mention of family hit a nerve and Luis winced. "Must be nice," he muttered before taking another swallow.

"To get my toenails painted on a Saturday afternoon?" Liam asked. He chuckled and Luis knew he was joking. "Never thought I'd be the kind of guy who enjoyed being a family man, but things change."

Luis nodded and took another drink. "It's Julia," he said after finishing his swallow. "She's still shaken up by what happened in the bunker—not that I blame her."

"Me, either. Sophie still has nightmares about Darcy Owens. Holly, too, though not as often. I guess her background in psychology helps her process things better. We've been trying to make sure Sophie feels safe, especially when she wakes up from those dreams. She screams…" Liam shook his head and took another slug from his bottle. "We did good getting that woman in jail."

Luis scanned the room. Had anyone heard their mention of Darcy and her arrest? No one was sitting nearby, much less cared about their conversation. "We did good, just not soon enough."

"What did you want to say about Julia? You said she was upset."

Shaking his head, Luis said, "It's nothing."

"It's just something, otherwise we wouldn't be having a beer."

He turned his attention to the television. An aftershave commercial filled the screen as the home team took the field to warm up.

Liam returned the conversation to Luis and Julia, and asked, "You like Julia, right?"

Luis drained his beer. "Sure. She's a good sheriff. When she worked at RMJ, she was a good teammate—the kind that always has your back, you know."

The game started again. Liam lifted the beer to his lips and took a swallow. Setting down the drink, he said, "What do you think about the game?"

He glanced at the screen. "Denver to win."

"You think Colorado? The team from New York is tough. Care to place a friendly bet?"

Bet. His heart began to race, and Luis's mouth went dry. His friend knew nothing about his past gambling problem…or what it had cost him in the end. "I never make a wager," he said. "Even on a sure thing like this."

The bartender pointed to the empty bottle. "You want another?"

"Better not." After all, he had to drive home. "I'll take an order of buffalo wings."

"Make that two," said Liam. He paused. "Where did you see Julia?"

"We met at the firing range," Luis said. "She wanted to practice shooting."

"How'd she do?"

Twisting the empty bottle between his palms, he thought for a moment before speaking. "Pretty bad, actually. She can't use her right hand at all, and her aim is way off when she shoots with the left."

"What will that mean for her work at the sheriff's office?" Liam asked. "She just took the job a few months ago."

It was the same question Julia had asked…and answered. If she couldn't hit a target, was her time in law enforcement over?

"All she needs is practice," said Martinez. "She still goes to physical therapy and occupational therapy. There's more the docs can do, but not yet. In time, she'll get better."

Two plastic baskets lined with wax paper and filled with steaming, sauce-covered wings were placed in front of Liam and Luis. Picking up a wing, Luis plunged the end into a small bowl of creamy ranch dressing.

Then again, Luis had problems of his own. Liam had unknowingly opened two of his wounds, and they were still raw. Luis never spoke to his family…and it was because of his addiction to gambling.

Sure, Marcus Jones—the leader of RMJ in Wyoming—knew about his past. But it was a secret closely guarded from everyone else, including Julia. Taking a bite of chicken wing, he chewed and tried to ignore the painful throbbing in his chest.

A large mirror hung above the bar, reflecting the entire room. The Watcher sat on a stool, gripping a bottle of beer. The burn of failure still stung. Everything had gone wrong, every step of the way, resulting in Darcy's arrest. Now she sat in jail. And it was all The Watcher's fault.

Then again, there were the two guys at the end of the bar. The conversation was, well, interesting and informative.

"It's Julia. She's still shaken up by what happened in the bunker—not that I blame her."

"Me, either. Sophie still has nightmares about Darcy Owens..." They tightened their grip on the bottle, breath catching in their throat. The guys continued. "We did good getting that woman in jail."

"We did good, just not soon enough."

Were they the ones who'd captured Darcy Owens? And who were the others? Holly? Sophie? Although the men knew about Julia—the new sheriff. So she'd been involved…

The Watcher's neck began to tingle, as if being watched from behind. A quick glance over the shoulder confirmed no one was there. But upon turning back, the Watcher's eyes were drawn to the glass. To her—the reason for the tingle on the back of the neck. Darcy Owens.

Nobody in the pub reacted, and that was when the Watcher knew two important things. No one else could see Darcy—she came only for The Watcher. And being in the pub at this exact moment wasn't a random coincidence. The Watcher had been called by Darcy again, just like before.

I need you, she said, her voice only a whisper. I need you to destroy them all. Do it for me.

And then, she was gone.

The Watcher's eyes moved to the table of boisterous men in the back of the bar and smiled. If Darcy wanted destruction, then the Watcher would destroy.

Chapter 2

Julia gasped and bolted upright in bed, her heart pounding against her chest. Sweat-dampened sheets were wound around her middle. The dream had been the same each night. The bunker. The pain. The blood. The moment when Julia became nothing.

The images faded and Julia rose from the bed. Black spots danced in front of her eyes. Drawing in a deep breath, she waited for her vision to clear. Julia was determined to put the past behind her—where it belonged.

Yet, the past continued to chase her down.

It was why she'd left Rocky Mountain Justice to become the sheriff of Pleasant Pines. Julia hoped that the change would be enough. It wasn't.

After changing into running tights, a sports bra

and a quarter-zip thermal top, Julia picked up her phone. She'd missed two calls from her mother.

It was 6:00 a.m. in Wyoming, so 8:00 a.m. in Connecticut and late enough in the morning to call her parents, especially since it was a Sunday. Yet, without her run Julia would be surly for the rest of the day. First things first.

Strapping her phone to her arm, she placed earbuds in her ears and opened the phone's music app. The opening chords of "Highway to Hell," her favorite AC/DC song, swelled around her. Stepping out of her home into the gray dawn, Julia paused on the front porch and inhaled deeply. The air was cool and smelled of pine.

After stretching and warming up, she started out at a jog. Her normal route took her from her home to Main Street. Around the town park, behind the hospital and back home. It was an easy four miles.

Most of the homes in her neighborhood were decorated for Halloween. Jack-o'-lanterns with wide smiles sat on porches. Scarecrows, arms out, stood in yards. Someone even hung tissue paper ghosts from a tree, and they flapped in the breeze.

As she ran, her body fell into a rhythm and her mind wandered. Her thoughts returned to the firing range. Immediately, her spine filled with the fiery indignation of failure. She hadn't even hit the target once.

Pushing her legs to go faster, as if she could outrun the fiasco, she began to sprint. One mile. A mile and a half. An ache crept into her joints, and a burning sensation pulled at her side.

Two blocks ahead, she spied the park, with the round gazebo at its center. The roof was made up of wooden shaker tiles that had turned a dusty gray with age and the weather. Three steps led to the deck and the base was surrounded by a latticework fascia. A bench lined the interior. Yet for Julia, the pergola looked like an oasis in the desert.

Legs trembling, she lurched across the damp lawn. Climbing the set of stairs, Julia stopped short.

A man was slumped over on the seat. With sandy blond hair, he wore a polar fleece jacket and jeans. She guessed his age to be midthirties. He was fit, yet his head leaned to the side and the angle of his neck was unnatural.

Pausing the music, she pulled her earbuds free.

"Hey, buddy." Julia's heartbeat still raced, and her voice was nothing more than a whisper. "You okay?"

He didn't answer. Somehow, she knew he wouldn't. Julia reached for the man's wrist. His skin was icy, the flesh flaccid. She felt for a pulse. Nothing.

How in the hell had a seemingly healthy man ended up dead on the bench in the gazebo?

She looked for signs of foul play. There was no bruising around the neck from strangulation. No bullet hole indicating that the man had been shot. Not even a knife wound, crusted over with blood.

It was simply as if he'd sat down on the bench and died during the night.

The death was almost like all the others…

Julia felt the faintest amount of pressure on her back, as if she'd been touched by a gaze. Peering quickly over her shoulder, she saw only an empty street and deserted park.

"Get a grip, McCloud," Julia said out loud. "Darcy Owens is in jail."

Clamping her mouth shut, she ran her tongue over her teeth. She was talking to no one—hardly a sign that she had a grip on anything at all. *Not to mention, it's not like Darcy could've broken out without my hearing about it!*

After removing the phone from her armband, Julia dialed the number to the sheriff's office.

The call was answered after the second ring. "Deputy Travis Cooper."

Travis Cooper had been with the Pleasant Pines sheriff's office for almost two decades. In fact, he had been the most likely candidate to replace the murdered Sheriff Haak…until the raid on the motorcycle club's compound went bad. Circumventing all law-enforcement protocol had cost Travis the job, but knowing Travis, she doubted that he regretted his decision at all.

He'd saved ten women being held against their will. One of the women was the daughter of Cassidy Frazier, Travis's girlfriend. And he'd served his community by getting drugs off the street.

Sometimes right was right.

If Deputy Cooper resented Julia for getting the position he wanted, thanks to her friend, council member Everly Baker, he never let on.

"Cooper," she said. "This is Sheriff McCloud. I know you're just finishing up your shift, but I need you at the town park. And get Doc Lambert over here pronto." Her training kicked in. There was evidence to gather. They needed to canvass for witnesses. Julia dared not touch the body without a pair of gloves—even to pat down the body to look for a wallet.

"Doc Lambert?"

"There's a body at the town gazebo. Male. Caucasian. Blond hair. Looks to be between thirty and thirty-five years of age. No visible sign of trauma. Not even a button out of place."

No visible sign of trauma. In other words, there was no reason the guy should be dead.

"I'll call Doc on my way over," he said.

Julia shifted her weight from one foot to the other. She knew her next question would sound crazy, yet she couldn't help but ask it. "Hey, Trav. She's there, right? Darcy is still in her cell."

"I got a report from the Northern Wyoming Correctional Facility this morning. They're keeping her in solitary."

Julia would rather that Darcy was locked away in a maximum-security prison, yet all people—even garbage like Darcy—had the presumption of innocence until proven guilty. For now, she was being housed in the regional jail and awaiting trial. Her tone softened a little. "Thanks, Trav." She added, "Tell Cassidy I'm sorry for keeping you late at work," before ending the call.

Julia moved to the steps. Arms folded across her

chest, she kept her posture rigid. As she stood there, Julia realized an ugly truth: death was once again stalking the peaceful town of Pleasant Pines. And now, finding out what happened to the guy on the bench was Julia's number-one priority.

Covers draped across his chest, Luis Martinez slept. A fuzzy paw nudged his forehead. "Go away, cat," he said, batting the feline to the floor.

Undeterred, Jinxy, Luis's eight-year-old tabby, jumped back on the mattress. This time when she smacked, her claws were out. A flash of pain filled his ear.

"What the hell?"

Picking up the phone, he checked the time—6:20 a.m. He cursed. "It's too damn early to be awake, and on a Sunday, too."

The cat purred indifferently.

"I know—you don't care."

Throwing back the covers, he dropped his feet to the bare wooden floor. Wearing only boxer shorts, he wiped sleep from his eyes as he wandered from his bedroom to the kitchen. As he suspected, Jinxy's dish sat on the kitchen floor, empty. After dumping food into the cat's bowl, Luis turned on the coffee maker and filled the reservoir with water.

His apartment was on the third floor of a brick building, original to the founding of Pleasant Pines. When he first moved in, he thought that living downtown would put him in proximity to restaurants and bars. Instead, he got a hardware store on the first floor, a dental office on the second and a town that rolled up its sidewalks at 8:00 p.m.

It wasn't exactly the thriving metropolis he'd hoped for.

Then again, coming to Pleasant Pines and taking the job with RMJ had been the fresh start that Luis needed. Maybe he didn't need restaurants and bars on his doorstep.

After brewing a cup of coffee, Luis sank onto the sofa and picked up his tablet computer. Using an app, he connected to the local newspaper, the *Pleasant Pines Gazette*. The lead story on this Sunday morning was about Darcy Owens. No surprise there. The story said that Darcy Owens had admitted to a single murder. William "Billy" Dawson. According to Owens, Dawson had found her in the woods and kept her captive in an underground bunker. Her imprisonment ended when Owens attacked her captor, decapitating the man.

Luis knew that fact too well. He'd been part of the team that had discovered Billy's dismembered corpse in the woods, miles outside of town. RMJ—Luis, Julia and all the others—had never been mentioned in the press…just like they had planned.

Darcy claimed self-defense. And since Luis had seen the bunker where Darcy had been held, he didn't doubt that her statement was true. But what of the other crimes of which she'd been accused? She stated that she'd lived her life with fragmented memories. The DA had brought in a psychologist to determine the validity of Owens's reports of "lost time." So far, the psychologist could neither confirm nor deny the truth of her claims.

"What crap," Luis grumbled, tossing his tablet aside. Certainly, Darcy was trying her best to appear ill, and therefore not responsible for the heinous crimes she'd committed. Over the years, she'd murdered dozens of men. She was the one who'd killed Sheriff Haak—with his own shotgun. She'd tried to hang both Holly Jacobs and Everly Baker. Kidnapped Liam's daughter, Sophie.

Attacked Julia with an axe and left her for dead.

No matter what she now claimed, Luis had seen enough of Darcy Owens in action to know that she had always been sure of what she was doing. With a shake of his head, he picked up his coffee cup and took a drink. "I hope nobody buys her story."

An approaching police car's siren let out a shrill blast. Luis ambled to a set of tall windows in the living room. With lights flashing, the cruiser was easy to find. It sped down Main Street and stopped at the town park, which was a block north of his apartment. Sipping from his cup, he watched and wondered what in the world was happening.

Blue and red lights strobed in the hazy morning light. Yet, it wasn't the car or the lights that captivated Luis's attention—it was the person who met the deputy. Julia McCloud.

He set aside the cup.

Even from a block away, he could tell that her pallor was gray. Her blond hair was damp with perspiration. What was happening at the park?

There was only one way to find out. Returning to his bedroom, he stepped into yesterday's jeans then shrugged on his Colorado Mustangs T-shirt and a flannel shirt, and finally slipped on a pair of shoes. Within a minute, he had jogged down the stairs and sprinted up the street.

Crime-scene tape had been wrapped around the posts that flanked the entrance to the gazebo. Julia was nowhere in sight.

Travis Cooper, a Pleasant Pines deputy, intercepted Luis on the sidewalk. Luis had already worked with the other man several times during the hunt for Darcy Owens. Rocky Mountain Justice preferred to work independently, but the agency never hesitated to partner with local law enforcement if that meant reaching their goal more effectively. "Julia call you, too?" Deputy Cooper asked.

Luis wasn't about to admit that he knew nothing about the situation. For sure, he would be told to move along. He gave a nod. "What's up?"

"There's not much to tell," said Cooper. "Except that the guy is dead."

Shaking his head, Luis made his way to the gazebo, where Julia and Doc Lambert were conversing. Their voices were barely above a whisper. Luis couldn't make out what they were saying, but he sure knew what they were talking about. Sitting on the bench, head lolled to the side, was the body.

Deputy Cooper had already told him what to expect, yet the sight brought Luis up short. Chest tight and head throbbing, he recalled walking into the bar at the Pleasant Pines Inn. There'd been a table full of men wearing mountain-bike gear.

The dead guy had been a part of the group.

"I saw him yesterday," said Luis.

Julia turned. Looking at Luis, she gaped. "What are you doing here and how in the hell do you know this guy?"

Luis ignored her first question and answered the second. "I don't know him personally, but I saw him. Yesterday at the pub at the Pleasant Pines Inn. He was there with a bunch of buddies—looked like they'd gone mountain biking."

Julia's color was still ashen. Ash-gray smudges darkened the skin under each eye. Had she slept at all? "That begins to solve the mystery of this guy's identity. Now all we need to figure out is why he's dead."

It wasn't exactly an invitation to join in the investigation. Still, Luis took a knee next to the corpse and gave voice to his initial thoughts. "There's no immediate physical evidence to make me think he's the victim of foul play." Moving closer, he continued, "There isn't even bruising around his neck or a contusion to his head." He stood and took a step back. "A heart attack?"

Doc Lambert said, "I'll conduct a full autopsy and then we'll know for sure."

Moving to the railing, Luis walked the perimeter of the gazebo, examining the expanse of lawn. "There are no tire tracks in the soil," he said. "Not even a furrow dug through the grass, where a body was dragged. Unless this guy was carried, he walked to this location and sat down."

"Why would he do that?" Julia asked.

Luis shrugged. "My guess is that he didn't feel well. Maybe he had chest pains and needed to rest." Returning to the body, he leaned in close and drew in a quick breath. The smell of meat, on the verge of turning rancid, filled his nostrils. Yet, underneath the stench, was another smell—subtle, antiseptic and sweet…yet unmistakable. "Whiskey," he said. "It seems like John Doe got good and drunk before he died."

"I'll run all toxicology reports during the autopsy. Might take a few days—or even a week—to get results back from the lab," said Doc Lambert.

A week was a long time to wait during an investigation into a suspicious death. Still, he didn't doubt that what the physician had said was true. Luis turned his attention back to the gazebo, reassessing the crime scene, wondering how many clues they might find about this John Doe…and how he died. He also knew that he didn't trust anyone to assist with the investigation, except himself. Now, here was the trick. How could he make sure that he stayed involved in the case?

Clearing his throat, Luis glanced over his shoulder at Julia. "You mind if I take a closer look at the body?" He stopped himself before offering to help, remembering how she'd reacted to his offer the day before.

"Suit yourself," she said, arms folded across her

chest. Luis figured that was as good of an invitation as he was going to get. "Got a pair of gloves, Doc?"

Doc Lambert withdrew several pairs of translucent gloves from his pocket and handed them to Luis. After pulling on the protective gear, he patted down the corpse. There was no wallet in the jacket pocket. None in the pants pocket, either. "Nothing," he said. "It looks like we have a John Doe."

Calling down to Deputy Cooper, Julia said, "I need you to secure a two-block radius. Don't let anyone in at all. Anything you find, you place in an evidence bag. After that, check the trash cans and see if a wallet was thrown away."

"Sure thing," said Cooper. "What else?"

"Get the other deputies over here. Have them bring the camera. I want photographs of everything."

Deputy Cooper nodded.

Luis returned to the victim and took out his phone to take photos. In his experience, every corpse had a story to tell. Too bad that this guy didn't have much to say…at least not yet.

"Have you been able to determine the time of death yet, Doc?" Julia asked, her arms still tightly folded over her chest.

At first, Luis had seen her stance as a defensive posture—body language meant to protect and ward off interference. Then he understood. She was cold—she was wearing running gear and had been sweating only moments before. While the morning chill had eased a bit, it was still far from warm.

Standing, he slipped off his flannel shirt. Holding it out to Julia, he said, "Here."

A beat passed. Then another. She reached for the shirt. Her fingertips grazed his knuckles and Luis's hand warmed. He tried to ignore the sensation of her touch while Julia worked her arms into the sleeves.

"Thanks." Then she turned and said, "Doc, if you and the deputies have this covered, I'm going to the inn and see if I can get an ID for John Doe. You got pics on your phone to show the staff at the inn?" she asked of Luis.

Rubbing his hand over her knuckles—the exact place she'd touched—he gave a terse nod. "Got 'em."

"Care to come with me?" she asked.

Luis never gave up when playing football in high school, or at community college. That inability to let go was what had made him a good cop. And a lousy gambler.

Then again, he already saw this case as his. So did he want to go with Julia? Without question. The need to know how the dead guy ended up in the gazebo was keen. Yet, he wasn't sure that being a part of the investigation was the best idea—not while his flesh still held the memory of Julia's touch.

Chapter 3

Peter Knowles sat behind his desk in the editor's office of the *Pleasant Pines Gazette*, staring at a blank computer screen. Finger hovering over the keys, he waited for inspiration to strike and unleash a torrent of words. They never came and the blank screen continued to chastise Peter for having nothing to say.

Early on a Sunday morning, the newspaper's headquarters was blessedly silent. Then again, they only operated with the smallest of staffs. There was a single photographer, who also wrote about high school sports. Two other reporters, a retired English teacher and a part-time novelist were paid by the article.

The *PPG* had been housed in the same building, five blocks from the town square for nearly a century. The walls were brick. The floor was wood. The radiator hissed and barely warmed the cavernous newsroom in the winter. Despite all its flaws, for Peter, this was home.

Searching for a topic for his column, Peter knew one thing for certain—more than half of the readers only wanted their biweekly copy of the *Pleasant Pines Gazette* to glance over the obituaries, local sports scores and bits of local gossip.

All of that changed when it was discovered that the sleepy town of Pleasant Pines had unknowingly been the home of a notorious serial killer—Darcy Owens. She had claimed several victims while living and working in town. Like a long-neglected houseplant, the community was thirsty for minute-by-minute updates as the story unfolded.

Peter had worked nonstop to provide the best information he could to the town. His hard work had paid off. Subscriptions quadrupled in a few short weeks. Peter started charging access to the paper's online site, something he never would have imagined possible.

Then, as quickly as the investigation began, it ended when the killer was arrested. The stories became less sensational as court proceedings and inconclusive psychological evaluations dulled the daily headlines. As Darcy Owens languished in a jail cell, Peter wondered if his newspaper would be her final victim.

The wail of a police siren drew Peter from his desk to the front window in the newsroom. Across the street sat the town park. Two deputies stood next to the gazebo—one of them had a roll of black-and-yellow crime-scene tape in hand. Doc Lambert, the town physician, was already on the scene. The new sheriff, Julia McCloud, was also there, dressed for running. A moment later, a big guy with a crew cut arrived. After speaking briefly to one of the deputies, Travis Cooper, the guy bounded up the steps.

Adrenaline surged until Peter's veins buzzed. His toe tapped and he slapped his fingers on the leg of his jeans. The jitters were his journalistic intuition, or so he always claimed. Slipping on a tweed blazer over his always pressed button-down shirt, he stepped into the early morning.

Mist rose from the grass that filled the town square. Loping across the street, Peter lifted his hand in greeting at the deputies. "Morning, fellas. What's going on?"

"Oh, it's you again," said Travis Cooper, rolling his eyes. "We can't say."

"Can't say because it's part of an investigation or because you don't know?"

"You need to move along," said the other deputy.

"Can I get at least a hint?" Peter asked. "Hey, who's the big guy I saw? The one with the crew cut?"

The deputies exchanged a narrow-eyed glance. For a reporter, that look was the death knell for any source. Still, something important had passed between the two men. What was it? Or, more importantly, how could Peter find out? "Can I at least talk to the sheriff? I know she's up there—I saw."

Deputy Cooper shook his head, saying nothing.

"One comment?" Peter asked, trying again.

"Move along." Deputy Cooper waved his arm, ushering Peter back the way he'd come.

"Sure thing," said Peter, then he headed back across Main Street and returned to the office. He'd given in to the deputies, yet he was undeterred. Taking a camera from the photographer's desk, he took up a position near the front window, prepared to watch and wait. Maybe standing at the window with a camera was a bit conspicuous, and he considered switching it out for his cell. Then again, the telephoto lens would get him better pictures than any he'd capture on a phone—and he was only conspicuous if he was caught. Stepping back into the room, Peter knew he wouldn't be seen from the street. He waited as an observer—a recorder of events—playing no role in the stories he told.

Within minutes, he was rewarded with action from the park. Julia and the dark-haired male descended the stairs and turned up Main Street. He snapped several pictures of the pair, focusing on the unknown male. A moment later, the coroner's van arrived. Two orderlies emerged, then they pulled out a stretcher, complete with an orange body bag on top, from the back of the van.

A body in the park?

Pressing his finger on the shutter button, Peter took several pictures of the orderlies maneuvering the gurney toward the gazebo.

Returning to his desk, he grabbed a pad of paper

and a pen. Scribbling furiously, he made a list of notes. *Dead person in gazebo? Identity?* Sheriff Mc-Cloud had given the dark-haired male access to the scene. That wasn't typical. Who was he? What role did he play? He paused, looking at the paper. Did he dare to make the link? Would it be ethical to assume a connection before having enough facts?

Then he thought about the increased readership. The online subscribers. The advertising accounts that were growing, alongside all the other regional papers that had already gone out of business and were long forgotten.

He wrote two words. *Darcy Owens?*

Staring at the notepad, Peter knew that he needed to follow up on the story about the dead guy in the park. And, really, it wasn't just about selling news-papers or even writing a decent story. Peter owed it to the town of Pleasant Pines to discover the truth about this newest death...and he'd walk through hell to find it.

The Watcher stood in an alleyway as the scene at the park unfolded. All the important players had arrived. The town doctor. The deputies. As a bonus, the editor of the *Pleasant Pines Gazette* had been snooping around. Even the sheriff was on hand—Julia McCloud.

A breeze blew around the building and ruffled the Watcher's hair. And there was a whispered voice in the wind.

She's the one to blame, said Darcy. *Julia McCloud.*

The Watcher pulled the phone. The screen was black, but in the reflection, they saw not their own face…but that of Darcy's.

Julia McCloud, the breeze repeated, as it pushed along a wayward leaf. *Start with her—and finish the rest.*

The Watcher entered Julia's name into a search engine. It didn't take long to find out everything there was to know about the sheriff of Pleasant Pines.

Julia McCloud—the middle daughter of three—had been born to a successful real-estate attorney and a socialite. The McCloud family owned homes in Nassau and Lake Tahoe but resided in coastal Connecticut.

Julia had excelled in both sports and academics as a high-school student, often having nice write-ups in the local paper. She'd turned down admissions at both Yale and Vassar to attend the US Military Academy at West Point. As a newly minted second lieutenant, she'd been accepted in the Army Ranger program, a feat for any soldier. She served in the military for ten years before attending one year of law school.

That was where the public trail for Julia McCloud ended, and it didn't pick up for several years, when she rematerialized as the sheriff.

It had been years since the Watcher had murdered anyone. And, in all honesty, the rush that came from killing had been forgotten. It was a power that throbbed into the core as the life force seeped from another.

The Watcher smiled at the perfection of the tableau.

How long would it take for them to make the connection? How long before they saw that this murder was like all the others committed by Darcy Owens?

And then what would the mysterious sheriff do?

Striding down the street, Julia tied the tail of Luis's shirt before tucking the ends into the newly formed waist.

"Look at you," said Luis, his tone teasing. "Taking a simple flannel shirt and turning it into high fashion."

She smiled, nudging him with her elbow. "Smart ass."

"Smart ass? Now I'm hurt. I gave you a compliment, and you call me names. I thought we were friends."

Friends. The word struck a chord in Julia's chest. They were friends, weren't they? That meant she owed him an explanation for what had happened at the firing range. "Listen," she said, rerolling a sleeve. "About yesterday. I overreacted. I shouldn't have gotten so defensive."

He waved away her almost apology. "I shouldn't have smothered you with offers of help. Let's just forget about yesterday and start over now."

"Sounds good," she said as the business district of Main Street ended and the road rose, ascending with the terrain. "And speaking of today, you think you can get some of the operatives from RMJ to look around the park? Give my deputies a hand?"

Luis removed a phone from the front pocket of his jeans. After typing out a message, he hit Send. "Done."

The Pleasant Pines Inn sat atop a rise. Built in the late 1800s, the building was made of wood and stone. Aside from having over two dozen guest rooms, there was also the pub, which doubled as the town's favorite watering hole, and Quinton's, a fancy restaurant.

Julia and Luis approached. A set of doors automatically opened.

The lobby was sparsely furnished with a set of wingback chairs covered in forest green upholstery, along with a wooden coffee table. One wall was filled with shelves of books. A brass plaque invited guests to borrow or leave a volume. A large fireplace filled another wall, and several logs were stacked on a grate, yet nothing burned. The front desk was to the left and even at this early hour—6:30 a.m.—it was manned by a young woman in a pressed shirt.

"Sheriff McCloud," the woman said effusively. Her name tag read Kate. "What brings you in at this early hour?"

Julia thanked the gods that ruled over small towns that the desk clerk recognized her on sight. "We need to talk to you about one of your guests."

"Do you have a name?" Kate asked.

Luis picked up where Julia left off. "A body was found at the park. He had no identification and the sooner we can figure out the man's name, the sooner we'll know what happened. Are any of your guests missing?"

Kate's eyes went wide. "A body? And you think… you think they stayed *here*?"

"We don't know what happened to this man and are only trying to get a name," said Luis. He held up his phone, with a photo of John Doe on the screen. "Can you take a look and let me know if you recognize this man."

Kate leaned in closer and stared at the screen. "It's kinda hard to tell, but he might be part of a big group that arrived two days ago to mountain bike. I mean, there's several guys but maybe…"

It was exactly what Luis had suspected. At least Julia knew that they were headed in the right direction. "Can you call a member of the party?" Julia asked.

"Sure. I mean, of course, we can help." Kate picked up the house phone and pressed several buttons.

Julia heard the line begin to ring.

"Hello," Kate said. "This is the front desk. There are some people who need to speak to you in the lobby." She paused a moment before saying, "Thank you," and placing the phone back on the receiver. "Someone will be over in a minute," she said to Julia and Luis.

Julia nodded her thanks, then stepped toward the fireplace, situated on the opposite side of the lobby. Luis followed, slapping the phone into his open palm. Several minutes later, a man walked into the lobby.

Medium build with dark hair and blue eyes. Julia put the man's age at early thirties. His hair stood on end and he wore a pair of jeans and an untucked T-shirt.

He went directly to the front desk. "I'm Sean Reynolds. Someone called and asked me to come to the lobby."

The desk clerk pointed to Julia and Luis. "Those two need to speak to you."

Rubbing his bleary eyes, the man approached. "What do you need?" he asked.

Julia stepped forward and held up her badge. "Mr. Reynolds, my name is Julia McCloud. I'm the sheriff in Pleasant Pines. I understand that you came here with a group of people, perhaps to mountain bike."

"So, what of it?"

"Is everyone in your party accounted for?"

Until now, Julia would have described the man's tone and demeanor as defiant, or at least unfriendly. Casting his gaze from Julia to Luis and back again, he changed to seeming bewildered and confused. "I'm sorry. What do you want to know?"

Luis lifted his phone and brought up the photo of John Doe. Holding up the picture, he asked, "Do you know who this is?"

"That's Tom Dolan, my brother-in-law. Why?"

"Have you seen him recently?" asked Luis.

"I spoke to him last night. We biked in the morning and then had late lunch in the pub. We went back to the bar for drinks last night, showed up around ten o'clock. The place was packed, and the party was pretty wild. I lost track of all the guys. But, I mean, we're all adults and staying at the hotel. It's not like anyone needed a babysitter or designated driver or anything. Tom never came back to the room."

Julia sucked in her breath, but Luis kept going.

"What do you remember about last night?" Luis asked.

"Tom was talking to a woman. She was tall. Blonde. I didn't get a good look at her, but she seemed…" Sean paused, then added, "Friendly."

"Friendly?" Luis echoed.

"Kissing Tom. She had her hands all over him. That kind of thing."

Julia flexed her hand as her missing fingers started to ache. The scar on her stomach itched.

"In fact, that's why I wasn't worried at all when he never came back to the room. Honestly, I thought he'd gone home with her. He hasn't been back. Do you know where he is? Are you here because you're looking for him?"

This part was never easy. "He was found this morning in the town gazebo. He'd passed away."

"No!" Sean was stricken. "He's gone? What happened to him?"

"I'm so sorry for your loss. And that's exactly what we are trying to find out," said Luis.

"Can you let us look around?" asked Julia. "See if there's anything that'll give us a clue about what happened?"

Sean nodded, wiping away tears. "My wife will be devastated."

Julia and Luis followed him across to his room on the first floor.

It was unremarkable—a standard hotel room. Two double beds. Single dresser with TV on top. Chair and desk. Adjacent bath.

Clothes littered the floor, and the room was filled with a not-so-fresh, locker-room aroma. Aside from the smell and clutter, Julia noted that one bed had been slept in, while the other was made. "What can you tell us about Tom's life? He's your wife's brother?"

"Tom lived in Atlanta. An architect. He just broke up with a long-term girlfriend—Tiffany Soames. He was real upset. Last night, I thought meeting someone new would be good for him. Damn it, I can't believe he's gone." Sean took a deep breath and shook his head.

"We are sorry for your loss," said Julia, echoing Luis's earlier words, feeling the man's pain as an ache in her chest. "Take your time."

Sean nodded and drew in several deep breaths. "Thanks."

"Do you have information for his parents? I can let them know what happened." Sean had a phone number and names in his phone and held up the screen for Julia to see. She tapped the information into her phone, saving it with her other contacts. "What about his ex-girlfriend? Was she as upset as Tom about the breakup?"

"I don't think so. She dumped him and married

some doctor." Sean pointed to a suitcase that sat open on the desk. "That's his stuff."

"When was the last time you remember seeing Tom?" Luis asked.

"To be honest, I'm not completely sure."

"Take your best guess," said Julia.

"Eleven. Maybe eleven thirty. It was definitely after ten thirty—we all did a shot then. I left the bar at midnight and Tom was already gone."

Luis removed a new set of latex gloves from his pocket—he'd probably gotten a couple of pairs from Doc Lambert before leaving the park—and began to sift through the contents of the bag.

"Bingo." He held up a black leather wallet. Odd that it would be in his suitcase and not with him.

Moving in closer, Julia watched as Luis opened the front flap. A piece of paper fell from the interior and slowly fluttered to the floor. Luis picked it up and cursed. It was half of a two-dollar bill—a calling card left by Darcy Owens with all her victims.

Julia stilled.

The MO with regard to the money had been kept pretty quiet—only the RMJ team and a few federal agents knew about it. Finding the half bill wasn't a coincidence—it was an undeniable link between Darcy Owens and the newest killing.

But how? Darcy was in custody.

Julia met Luis's gaze and saw her deepest fear reflected in his eyes. She knew he felt the same way she did, no matter how much he would try to deny it to her.

She might be behind bars, but somehow, Darcy had managed to kill again. And Julia couldn't even begin to imagine how you stopped a murderer who was already behind bars.

But one thing was certain. She was damn well going to find out.

Chapter 4

Cold sweat broke out on Luis's body. Sure, on some level he suspected that there might be a connection between Tom Dolan and the other victims of Darcy Owens. But he never imagined it'd be so concrete as the money, a clue too blatant to brush off as coincidence, a clue kept quiet enough it would be difficult to claim that the killer was a random copycat.

Removing his phone, he snapped several pictures of the wallet and the bill, ripped in half, that was lying on the ground. In that same split second, Luis knew that something wasn't quite right.

"Why is the wallet here?" he asked. "And not with Tom?"

"We all charged drinks to the room," Sean said.

"Seemed easier than cash or keeping track of a credit card."

It also meant that the killer had been in Tom's hotel room, as well—and they might have left a trail of evidence behind. "This place needs to be dusted for prints," said Luis.

Julia was already sending a text. "I'll have the deputies come over as soon as they're done at the park."

"Sean, I hate to do this to you, man," said Luis. "You're going to have to keep out of this room while it's searched."

"I mean, whatever you need, you got from me." Sean swallowed and blinked hard, holding back tears. He blew out a gust of air. "I guess I have to tell the other fellas about Tom. It sucks. Just do me one favor—find out what happened to him. He was a good guy and deserved better than, well, whatever. You know."

"We know," said Julia. "And stay close to the inn. We'll need to get official statements from everyone in your party."

"Sure, we'll be here."

They all left the room and Luis, still wearing gloves, closed the door behind him. Walking down the hallway, the thrill of the investigation sparked in his veins. "We need to get more than fingerprints from the room," he whispered, to avoid being overheard. "The killer was in this hotel. There might be other witnesses. Or video of the crime."

"That means getting a look at the hotel's surveillance videos. Who know what we can find that would be useful?" said Julia as they approached the front desk.

"May I help you?" the clerk asked. Kate added, "I talked to the owner and he said to assist you in any way possible."

"Can we see video footage from last night?" Luis asked.

The young woman pointed to a door that was set behind the front desk. "We have monitors in there."

In a large hotel, such as one found in downtown Denver, Luis would've expected to find a separate suite for security purposes. But he wasn't in Denver anymore and there was a lot he still had to get used to. A set of three boxy monitors sat on a table in the back office. Each screen was broken into four separate pictures. The hallways, both upstairs and downstairs, had been covered from three different angles. There were two shots of the lobby. One was of the front entrance, along with live video of both the restaurant and the pub.

Luis asked, "Can you show us video for the lobby outside of the pub from eleven o'clock until midnight?"

"Sure thing," said the clerk.

Kate typed on a keyboard attached to one of the monitors. The screen went black for a moment before being filled with images of late-night partygoers. They stared at a smaller screen that was filled with a grainy image of a doorway to the pub. The time stamp on the video clicked by, minutes passing in seconds.

People came and went. A man exited the pub. The time was listed as 11:47 p.m.

"Stop," said Luis.

"Can you back up the video and slow the frame?" Julia asked.

The desk clerk rewound the video and slowed the image as it replayed. The door opened and a man stepped out. His back was to the camera that was across the lobby. He had a similar build to Tom Dolan. Was it him? Luis couldn't be sure.

Then the man looked toward the front desk, almost directly at the camera.

"It's him," Julia said, breathless. "It's Tom."

Tom Dolan stood in the lobby, swaying slightly, as he shifted from foot to foot. "He's alone, though."

"It looks like he's waiting for something," said Julia. "Or someone."

She'd been right. The pub's door opened a second time and a tall woman exited.

The woman's head was down, a tumble of blond hair forming a curtain around her face. "Damn," said Luis. "It looks like Darcy."

"You can't even see her face," said Julia, her tone snappish.

"True," said Luis. He watched as the couple walked through the lobby and disappeared from the camera's view. "But the coloring and build are the same."

"Does another camera pick them up anywhere else?" Julia asked.

"Let me see," said Kate. After a few keystrokes, she brought up video from the hallway outside the room. Tom and the woman entered his hotel room and exited a few minutes later. He staggered as he walked, his pixelated face showing a vacant expression. His female companion appeared to be holding him up as they walked away.

"Look up. Look up. Look up," Luis said, trying to coax the woman's image.

She never did. He assumed that the woman was aware of the cameras in the hotel and how to avoid being caught on tape. The couple walked out of the camera's view and disappeared. Luis hadn't seen everything, but he'd seen enough to know that they had a problem.

One woman—namely, Darcy Owens—was in custody for committing several serial killings. Another murder had taken place, and the circumstances were eerily similar to what had occurred before. Beyond that, the description for both Darcy and Tom's companion matched.

He held up his phonc with the email address for Katarina, RMJ's communications expert, on the screen. "Can you send all of the video to this address? Along with everything you recorded last night."

"Sure thing." Kate typed on the keyboard.

Luis turned to Julia. "This woman had to arrive sometime. Even if she avoided all the cameras, maybe we'll get lucky and find a license plate for her car."

"Done," said Kate. "You can stay here and look through the videos as long as you want, but I have to get back to the front desk. If you need anything else, just holler."

"Thanks for your help," said Julia at the same moment her cell pinged with an incoming message. Glancing at the phone, she read the text. "It's Chloe. She wants to meet at your office about Tom Dolan."

Chloe Ryder was the DA for Pleasant Pines, and the person who'd hired RMJ to be a part of the Darcy Owens case.

He wasn't surprised that Chloe knew about the case, yet the fact that she wanted to meet at RMJ's office meant that the agency was about to be officially involved in this newest investigation.

He lived for moments when all the pieces of a puzzle came together to form a picture that was the truth. And Luis was the logical choice of operatives—after all, he'd spent years as a detective.

Rolling his shoulders back, Luis realized that he'd been absorbed in his own thoughts for too long. For her part, Julia didn't seem to have noticed. After tapping a message into her phone, she glanced up. "Two deputies are on their way to dust Tom Dolan's room for prints. At some point, all the guys who traveled with Tom have to be interviewed. That's a lot of work for a small department. My guess is that Chloe wants RMJ to assist the sheriff's office. We have this case but several other open investigations, so I'll welcome the help."

It's what he'd already guessed, so nothing new. "When's the meeting?"

"Everyone's there now."

He moved to the door. Julia remained where she stood.

"What're you waiting for?"

She held up her phone. The contact information for Tom Dolan's parents was on the screen. "You ever make one of these calls before?"

"Sure," he said. During his years with the Denver PD, he'd contacted dozens of families about deceased loved ones. It was his least favorite part of the job. "They're a gut punch, I'm not going to lie."

"I guess that explains why I feel sick." She paused. "I mean, I've lost people in combat, but it was never my job to tell the family. I only spoke to them after they knew."

"Want some advice?"

"Not usually," she said, giving him a small smile. "But this time, I'll take it."

"Be honest, professional and kind. That's what I always tried to do."

"Honest. Professional. Kind. I think I can pull it off."

"Of course, you can," he said, dropping his hand on her shoulder. "You want a minute?"

Julia inhaled deeply. After blowing out her breath in a single huff, she nodded. "Thanks."

"I'll wait in the lobby," said Luis as he hooked his thumb toward the door.

He paused on the threshold, glancing once over

his shoulder. Standing with her back to Luis, Julia had the phone pressed to her ear. "Mr. Dolan, my name is Julia McCloud. I'm the sheriff in Pleasant Pines, Wyoming. I'm afraid I have some terrible news."

Stepping out of the room, Luis's chest got tight as it expanded with pride for Julia and her demeanor. Back in the day, she'd been a hell of a soldier. Then, at RMJ, she'd been second to none. Now, she was proving to be a capable and compassionate sheriff.

In short, anything she touched turned to gold.

It was the exact opposite of Luis, who'd pissed away every opportunity he'd ever been given. Sure, he'd landed on his feet with RMJ. But what was stopping him from screwing up his life yet again?

To call the Wyoming headquarters of RMJ an office didn't do the space justice. Half a mile from the county office building, where the sheriff's office was located, RMJ had renovated a nineteenth-century home. From the outside, the house was unremarkable. Gabled roof. Dormer windows. Dentils along the eaves.

Yet, Julia had worked inside that building and knew that looks were deceiving.

Planted in the uppermost gable was a high-powered camera that recorded images in 360 degrees. There was also a microphone sensitive enough to pick up a conversation from two blocks away.

Getting into the building was a feat in itself. The door wasn't controlled by a simple lock and key. Instead, only those with the correct biometrics could gain access. Since she'd left the agency several months ago, there was no way that Julia could get past the front door. That was how secure they were.

But she was with Luis. As they stood on the stoop, his face was scanned, and his fingerprint was verified. The front door opened with a click and they entered a space that at one time had been a foyer.

It was now a steel holding cell. It took only seconds more for Luis to pass all the security devices, and soon they were sitting in a conference room on the first floor.

The team was already gathered and were sitting around a wooden conference table. Holding her breath, she waited for a pang of regret to fill her chest. After all, she'd been a part of this team for years.

No strong emotions rose to the surface…save for an affection for the people in the room. That, along with a burning to desire to find out what really happened to Tom Dolan…and why.

Marcus Jones, bald with a dark brow, was the operative in charge of the RMJ office in Wyoming. He sat at the head of the table. A former FBI agent, Marcus had joined the team in Denver after RMJ's hunt for a Russian drug lord, Nikolai Mateev, had intersected with an investigation run by the FBI.

Next to Marcus sat Chloe Ryder, the DA. She must have also been escorted inside by someone else. Even on a Sunday, she was dressed for business in jeans and button-down blouse. Liam Alexander and Wyatt

Thornton—both operatives with RMJ—sat on one side of the table. The communications expert, Katarina, sat at the table's foot, leaving two seats open opposite Wyatt and Liam.

Julia took one chair; Luis, the other.

Chloe started the meeting. "Now that we're all here, I'd like to thank everyone for showing up on such short notice. I don't like dead bodies showing up in my town. Everyone's still on edge with what happened with Darcy Owens and this newest case could cause a panic."

"We don't even have a cause of death yet," said Wyatt. "Until Doc Lambert's done an autopsy, we won't know what we're dealing with."

"I'll make some calls to Laramie. There are folks at the attorney general's office who owe me a few favors. I'm not making any promises, but maybe we can get the results back in a few days."

Julia glanced at Luis. Phone in his hand, he sent a message. "I think we have an idea of what we're dealing with. Katarina, I just sent you a photograph. This was found in the wallet of the victim, Tom Dolan."

"Got it," said Katarina. She pulled out a keyboard that was hidden in the table. With a few keystrokes, a screen lowered from the ceiling. "And this is the picture Luis just sent." The screen filled with four separate windows of the same image from different angles. "Damn," whispered Katarina. "A two-dollar bill, torn in half."

"The calling card from Darcy Owens," said Wyatt, stating both the obvious and unbelievable.

"Should we assume our victim—" he paused "—was murdered and there's a link to Darcy?"

"Tom Dolan," she said, filling in his name. Julia didn't want to forget that the reason they were meeting had been a person with a life. "An architect from Atlanta, in Pleasant Pines on the weekend because his ex-girlfriend had just married another guy." Chloe might've brought everyone together, but this death had occurred in Julia's jurisdiction—the case was hers. She continued, "As far as the cause of death, I don't want to assume anything. Still, the ripped two-dollar bill is a strong link to Darcy Owens. We can't ignore that connection."

"Agreed," said Chloe. "I wanted RMJ involved with the investigation when it was only a suspicious death, but now I'm going to insist on having their help."

Chloe was the youngest district attorney in Pleasant Pines history and the first woman to hold the job. There was a lot to admire about her, yet the sting of insult warmed Julia's cheeks. Then again, she knew the truth—the Pleasant Pines sheriff's office was small—only two full-time deputies, two part-time deputies, an office manager and Julia. Already, there were several angles associated with the death of Tom Dolan and plenty of leads to follow. "We should start by looking into the background of the victim. Tom Dolan's brother-in-law, Sean Reynolds, didn't know of anyone who might want to hurt him. But that doesn't mean he's right," she said.

"Or honest," Wyatt added.

"I can definitely use some bodies to find out all we can about Tom," she said. "And if he has any connection to Darcy Owens."

"I can take care of Tom's daily life," said Katarina, already typing on the keyboard. "I'll look at his social-media accounts, get an idea of his spending habits, the works."

"There's something else I'd like you look into. The desk clerk at the inn sent you two emails with clips from last night."

"Got those, too."

"Can you bring up the shorter clip on the main screen?"

Katarina entered a few keystrokes and the grainy image from the hotel's security camera began to play.

Luis narrated as the film continued. "This is Tom Dolan, the victim, outside the pub."

"Was he one of the mountain bikers who were there yesterday?" Liam asked. "He looks familiar."

Luis nodded. "He was." On the screen, Tom stood, swaying slightly. "And this," he continued, "is an unknown blonde female, who Tom's friend described as 'friendly.'" He hooked air quotes around the last word. "Kissing him. Running his hands over his chest."

"Damn," Wyatt whispered. "If I didn't know better, I'd say that was Darcy Owens."

"We noticed the similarities, too." Julia opened and closed her injured hand as the couple staggered down the hallway. The vantage point on the screen changed. Tom and his companion stood in front of the door to his room. "Our victim goes into the room with the blonde. I don't want to assume anything—perhaps there's another reason that Tom had half of a two-dollar bill in his wallet. But this time would give the woman an opportunity to plant the bill, if she wanted." The door opened a moment later. "Tom and his lady friend then leave the hotel and Tom isn't seen again until this morning, when he's a corpse."

"And never once do we see the woman's face," said Marcus.

"Correct," said Julia. "Katarina, can you look through the video, see if you can catch a reflection? Can you check the footage from the other email, as well?"

"I'll look through it all and see what I can find."

"I have my guys searching Tom's room right now," Julia continued, moving the meeting along. "I hope we can get the woman's prints off of something. Then again, she avoided all security cameras in the hotel, so I'm not hopeful that she accidentally touched a surface." Her phone began to vibrate with an incoming call. She glanced at her phone. Caller ID read Mom.

Damn. She hadn't gotten a chance to return her mother's call. After sending the call to voice mail, Julia turned back to the meeting. "I'll coordinate all parts of the investigation, and right now we aren't going to presume anything about this case. We don't even have a cause of death yet," Julia continued.

"I'm a tracker, not a cop," said Liam. "And I get that if we make assumptions, then we find clues that fit our narrative. But how many more clues do we need? Even without finding the two-dollar bill, ripped in half—the same damn thing Darcy left with each of her victims—I'd say there were a lot of links between her victims and this one."

"I agree," said Wyatt.

Julia knew Wyatt's story well. When Wyatt Thornton had been an FBI agent, working on finding an unknown serial killer in Las Vegas, his career had been ruined when the wrong person was charged. After leaving the Bureau, he moved to Pleasant Pines. Even if Wyatt was done with law enforcement, the killer wasn't through with him. A body had been found on his property, and Wyatt was drawn into the investigation. That killer was Darcy Owens. She'd taken the life of the long-time town sheriff, and damn near killed Wyatt's girlfriend, Everly Baker. "Is it a copycat? Or the accessory who helped her get the job at the White Wind?"

Julia didn't like either option, yet she knew that Wyatt and Liam were most likely right. Turning to Chloe, she said, "Darcy's in jail, waiting for trial. You've had her interviewed by a psychologist. What has your office learned?"

"Not much," she said. "She's admitted to killing William Dawson. But that's it."

"Could Darcy have shared the facts about the two-dollar bill with someone else?" Julia asked. "Maybe someone who's visited her?"

"Beyond her attorney and psychologist, she hasn't had any visitors. Whatever she says to her attorney is privileged, but we have audio from all her interviews with the psychologist. Nothing's been mentioned about the bills or getting a message to anyone else."

"The attorney?"

"He's a straight shooter," said Chloe. "He'd never enter into a conspiracy to commit murder."

"Internet access?" Wyatt asked. "Could she be sending emails?"

"None at all," said Chloe. "She's never around other inmates, either. So it'd be impossible for her to pass a message to one of them."

After a beat, Marcus asked, "What do you want from RMJ, Julia?"

"I need everyone in Tom's group interviewed," said Julia. "Hell, I need to find everyone who was in that pub last night."

Marcus said, "RMJ can handle the interviews. Liam. Wyatt. Me. We're on it."

"And Luis?" she asked.

"Luis will stay with you. He'll be RMJ's lead."

The last thing Julia wanted was for Luis to be her partner on the case. It had nothing to do with his investigative skills. In fact, his years as a detective in Denver made him the perfect investigator for the murder case.

But both Luis and Julia knew she was injured—maimed for life. She also knew she needed help with the investigation, just like she might need help with her job. It was just that she loathed the idea of Luis seeing her as weak…or needy. In fact, knowing that Luis pitied her might cause the biggest wound of them all.

Chapter 5

Peter Knowles sat at his desk, a phone to his ear. On the other end of the call was the local funeral director, Cheryl Sams.

"I'm working on the next issue of the paper," he said. "And am wondering if you've got an obit ready for me?"

"An obituary?" Her voice rose with the question. "Why would I have one of those? Who died?"

Peter wasn't surprised that Cheryl knew nothing of the body. But his lack of shock left his stomach and chest burning. He reached for a bottle of antacids at the back of his desk and popped two in his mouth. Chewing, he said, "The coroner's van was at the gazebo first thing this morning."

"Nobody called me to pick up a body. I wonder who it is? And what happened?"

What happened, indeed. "Let me know if you get the call. I'll save space in the section." Then he hung up.

Peter had been honest with Cheryl…and he hadn't. He was working on the next edition of the *PPG.* Yet he knew there'd been something suspicious about the death. He just needed Cheryl to confirm that the stiff wasn't a local. If it had been, a protocol would have been followed that included Doc Lambert contacting the funeral home to collect the body as soon as the family had been notified.

Peter still knew he was on the trail of a story, and a good one at that. The lack of statements from officials—Doc Lambert and Sheriff McCloud, to name two—didn't discourage him. Quite the opposite—the hunt for facts left him energized.

It was almost like the series he wrote back in the early 1990s as a reporter embedded with the troops back when he worked for a major New York newspaper. A drug cartel was sneaking heroin into the country through troops rotating home—some of the soldiers were unsuspecting, others less so. The articles placed Peter on the short list for the Pulitzer, a prize he never won.

Then life brought him back to his hometown of Pleasant Pines, the last place he wanted to be. Yet, for decades, he'd made it work. And because of Darcy Owens, he actually had news to report…or he used to, at least.

Still, there were other stories out there—like what had gone on in the park this morning?

The camera sat on the edge of his desk and he removed the memory card, taking only seconds to plug it into his computer. He opened a file, and his screen filled with dozens of thumbnail shots from this morning. He scanned the images. After selecting one, he double-clicked.

The entire picture filled his computer screen. Sheriff McCloud, arms folded across her chest, looked at the dark-haired man, who was in profile. Even in the picture, it was impossible to miss the woman's injured hand. Peter had seen more than enough mangled flesh while covering the first Gulf War to write a book on battle wounds.

He recalled the town council meeting when Sheriff McCloud's employment was announced. At that time, her hand had been in a bandage and he assumed the injury was minor. Looking at it now, he knew he'd been wrong.

What had happened to Julia? And without the use of her hand, could she really protect and serve the people of Pleasant Pines?

Yet, there were other mysteries to be solved.

Who had died at the park, and what had killed them?

And who was the guy with dark hair?

Peter opened another picture. This time, the dark-haired guy was staring straight at the camera, almost as if he could see Peter at the window.

"Let's find out who you are," he said, copying and

cropping the photo. He pasted the picture into a web browser and conducted an image search. The first photos to appear were of an actor, grown now, who used to star in a popular kids show that aired in the 1990s. He could see the resemblance, certainly, but it wasn't the same guy.

Sighing, Peter scrolled. The amount of red carpet moments was endless.

His finger stopped. Leaning toward the computer, he stared at a picture from one of the Denver papers.

Bingo.

The headline read, Detective Connected to Deaths of Quarterback, Russian Drug Lord.

There, on the front page of the paper, was a photo of the dark-haired man. Flanked by two uniformed cops, he was walking up the stairs to police headquarters. The caption under the photo read Detective Luis Martinez, a Twelve-Year Veteran of the Denver PD, on the Way to Meeting with the Chief of Police."

Luis Martinez. At least Peter had a name to go with the face.

Grabbing a pen and paper, Peter pulled both to him. Sure, he could take notes on his phone or just snap a picture of the screen. But he was old school—or maybe just old—and therefore set in his ways.

On his first day of J-school in 1984, a professor had stood in front of the class. The man had a mane of white hair and a tweed jacket, almost like Mark Twain had come back from the dead. Holding a pen in one hand and a pad of paper in the other, the professor had proclaimed, "There are three things every journalist needs. A pen. And paper."

Lifting his hand, Peter asked, "What's the third thing?"

"An unwavering desire for the truth. Followed by the ability to ask a question."

Decades later, technology had changed. But he hadn't. He still burned with a need for the truth; and to this day, he'd never been afraid to ask a question.

Turning his attention back to the article, Peter noted the date—two years ago—along with the reporter's name. He read the article. Luis Martinez, a decorated police detective, had been involved in the murder investigation of the Colorado Mustangs quarterback. There were ties between the killing and the Russian Mafia. A performance-enhancing drug that could slip through the league's testing was linked to the death, as well. In the end, a Denver physician was charged with the murder and an abandoned warehouse had burned to the ground. The owner of the Colorado Mustangs, Arnie Hatch, had also been charged as an accessory and coconspirator. The trial was short and the outcome brutal, at least for Hatch. He'd been convicted on all counts, and to this day was still serving time in prison.

Luis Martinez, lead detective on the murder case, had been put on administrative leave—not given a medal or a raise.

Why?

Time for a call. It was answered after the second ring.

"Smitty," said Peter, using the nickname he'd given Scott Smith when they were both beat reporters at a small paper in Boise, Idaho. Scott Smith now worked as a news director for a TV station in Denver. "It's Peter. Peter Knowles."

"I know who this is," said Scott with a laugh. "Who else would use that horrible nickname?"

"Been a long time since the days in Boise."

"Nineteen-eighty-nine."

"Christ on a cracker, no wonder I feel old. I am." The professor in J-school had told the class that there were three things a journalist needed to succeed at their job—four, if you counted the ability to ask a question.

But there was something he forgot to mention—a need to work sources. It was why Peter called Cheryl Sams at the funeral home earlier and why he was on the phone with his buddy now. "Listen, I wouldn't bother you on Sunday if it wasn't important. I'm doing background on a former Denver detective—left the force about two years back—and I have some questions."

"Sure thing," said Scott. "Your call got me out of looking at napkins for my daughter's wedding reception."

Seriously? Scott's baby girl was getting married. Maybe Peter *was* old. "The detective's name is Luis Martinez. He led up the murder investigation for the Mustangs QB. From an article I found, two years back, looks like the investigation had a lot of moving parts. Then, Detective Martinez gets put on administrative leave, never to return to the force."

"You know that two years is like two decades in the media world, but I do recall that case. It was big news. Lots of heads rolled."

"Including the detective? Was he a scapegoat for something?"

"Best I can remember, the cop and the QB were friends from early on. They grew up on the same block, that kind of thing. There was some scuttlebutt about the fact that the detective shouldn't have been involved in the case. Or at least he should've disclosed the friendship, which wasn't exactly a secret."

Peter wrote and spoke at the same time. "Is that enough for someone to get canned in Denver?"

"Not really," said Scott. "But there were rumors—unsubstantiated, mind you—that the detective was a suspect in the killing. Again, rumor, but he was told to leave the case alone and he didn't."

"Any other rumors?" Peter asked, flipping the pad to a clean sheet of paper.

"The theory was that the detective had a lot of gambling debts. But the guy left the force, and we found a new story to follow like a gaggle of geese." Scott paused. "What's this about, anyway?"

"Detective Martinez has turned up in Pleasant Pines and I want to know why he's here."

"We-e-ell..." Scott drew out the word.

"'Well' what?" Peter asked, knowing that there was more.

"There was also a rumor about a shadow agency involved with the case."

"Shadow agency?" Peter wrote the words on the page, then circled them twice. "What's that?"

"You know, private security but on steroids. They kind of work with the government. They kind of work for themselves."

Peter stared at the door, seeing nothing. What would a shadow agency be doing in Pleasant Pines, Wyoming?

From the other end of the call, Peter heard voices in the background—female and upset.

"Listen," said Scott, "I have to go. Be on the lookout for the wedding invite."

"I'll be honored to attend. I'll even wear a tie," Peter joked. He never wore a tie.

"Tie? You'll need a tux for this one."

Tux? Ugh.

"Tell me one thing," said Scott. "How many freaking shades of pink exist in the world?"

"A million," said Peter. "There are a million shades of pink."

"And then some," said Scott before hanging up the phone.

Peter reviewed his pages of notes about Luis Martinez—some facts verified, others little more than innuendo. But his eye was drawn again and again to two words. *Shadow agency.*

It was then that he realized an important truth. There was a sixth element to be a journalist. *Never ignore a story.*

Luis Martinez might be the key to one of the biggest stories in the history of Pleasant Pines.

Julia, along with the rest of the team, had put in a long day with the investigation. Interviews had been conducted and searches had taken place. Still, they were no closer to discovering what had happened to Tom Dolan. As the sun set, she sent the team home.

Now, hours later, Julia sat at her kitchen table, surrounded by files, photographs and statements. Tom Dolan seemed to be a genuinely nice guy. His friends were loyal. His parents were kind. Hell, even his ex-girlfriend was distraught over his death. He didn't have any outstanding debts. He donated to charities and volunteered his time at a local foodbank.

There was nobody who wanted to harm him… yet, someone had.

So far, Doc Lambert didn't have a cause of death. Despite the fact that both Julia and Chloe had asked that a blood-tox report be expedited, the state labs had made no promises for timely results.

Which meant what?

Julia had no motive. No suspect. No cause of death.

But there was more to the case. There had to be.

The two-dollar bill, ripped in half, and found in Tom's wallet, was a direct link to Darcy Owens. Julia stared at a picture of the half bill. The image blurred as the room around her faded to nothing. Trapped in her mind, her thoughts returned to the bunker. Darcy blocked the only exit. Drunk on her own hubris, Julia thought that she could outsmart the serial killer and somehow get to her firearm. Julia had lunged for her gun. With a gleeful look in her eye, Darcy had brought down an ax on Julia's hand. *Thwack.*

Fire danced along Julia's palm as the photograph slipped from her grasp and fluttered to the floor. Bending to pick it up, she froze, her heartbeat racing.

Had a face been peering at her through the window over the sink?

Julia moved to the sliding glass door at the back of her house. The motion-sensitive light was dark. She flipped on a set of floodlights that lit her backyard. Bare trees and the remnants of last summer's garden were visible from where she stood...but nothing else.

Her own reflection wavered in the glass. Had that been what she'd seen? Had Julia simply caught a glance of her own reflection? Still, she should at least walk the perimeter of her property. She had neighbors who counted on her to keep them all safe.

Before she could move, her phone trilled with an incoming call.

Julia lifted the cell from the table.

Her mother.

Damn. She hadn't called her back. It was after 9:00 p.m. local time, which meant it was after 11:00 p.m. in Connecticut, and well past her mother's bedtime.

Swiping the call open, she spoke without greeting. "I am so sorry for not calling you back. I got all your messages, but today got away from me."

"Julia. Honey. I'm just so glad to hear your voice.

I was starting to get worried. Well, I'm a worrier by nature," she said, and gave a small laugh. "So I guess that's no surprise."

"I know, Mom. I should've at least sent a text but today got out of hand."

"Oh, dear. A Sunday. What happened?"

"There was a death in town."

"And you have to deal with it?"

"Well, yeah, Mom," said Julia. "I mean, I am the sheriff."

"I know. I know. I just wish after everything that happened last time you would've come home."

They'd had this conversation more than once. During those first weeks of her recovery, Julia's parents had come from Connecticut and stayed in Wyoming. Her mother had been white-faced with worry and her father had chuffed like an angry horse.

As they left, Julia's mother had pleaded with her daughter to come home. Julia had refused, but her mother was undeterred.

After walking to the adjacent living room, Julia flopped down on the sofa. How could a few minutes on the phone with her mother drain her energy faster than a whole day of working a case?

"You know your father was talking to one of his friends at the club this morning."

"Uh-huh."

Her mother continued, "He went to law school with your father and works for the government. Well, as it turns out, he's recently been named as the US Attorney for the District of Connecticut. Well, I don't have to tell you that's an impressive and important job."

"Uh-huh."

"And he asked about you. He said he could use people in his office like you."

Julia sat up taller. "Like me?"

"I thought that'd get your attention. Anyway, he likes to hire attorneys who attended military academies. Says they're more disciplined than the most."

"I did go to West Point. There's one thing you're missing, Mom. I'm not an attorney."

"Yet—"

Julia spoke over her mother. "And I don't want to be an attorney, ever."

"I know that's what you say. Think of it this way—you didn't like the idea of law school when you thought you were going to work with your father. Maybe that's why you only lasted a year there. I understand that real-estate law isn't for everyone. I also know that you want to be one of the good guys—working to keep us all safe and serving justice and stuff like that."

Stuff like that?

Her mother continued, "Here's where this is the perfect plan. You can still serve the community, but instead of going to war or facing down criminals during an investigation, which are all dangerous, you could make sure all the bad guys get sent to jail. Doesn't that sound better?"

No, it did not.

Julia looked at her mangled hand. Then again,

maybe her mother had a point. "Law school's expensive, Mom. And it's hard to pay for things if I don't have a job—which I won't if I leave Wyoming and finish two years of law school."

"Live here—you can even move into the carriage house for privacy. Plus, your grandmother left you all of that money. You haven't touched a cent."

Julia worked her jaw back and forth. "I'll tell you what, Mom. I'll think about it."

"That's all I ask, honey. Well, now that I've talked to you and I know you're okay, I can at least get some sleep."

"Thanks for calling, Mom. I miss you."

"Love you. Bye."

Stretching out on the sofa, Julia reached for the remote and turned on the TV. She was still wearing Luis's flannel shirt. Tucking her nose into the collar, she inhaled deeply. His scent swirled around Julia, until she was light-headed with the smell.

But there was nothing to be gained by an attraction—much less a relationship—with Luis. In fact, if things went bad, she'd lose more than a lover—she'd lose a good, loyal friend, as well. Turning her attention to the TV, she flipped through the channels. As she was lying on the sofa, Julia admitted that her mother's plan had merit. The job of a prosecuting attorney would check a lot of boxes. Yet, was she ready to make such a drastic change? A killer prowled the streets of Pleasant Pines, she couldn't ignore that fact. Yet, her mangled hand still smarted. Her sleep was haunted with nightmares. Her aim with a firearm was horrible.

Would she ever be whole again? Would she ever escape the past enough to build a future in law enforcement?

And if not, then what?

Thank goodness she didn't have to answer the question tonight.

Settling on a hockey game, she tucked a pillow under her head and let her mind wander.

But she returned to the same question again and again. Was now the time to make a move? Was it time to abandon her quest for justice…and was she on a mission she'd never be able to finish?

Holding the sensor for the motion light, the Watcher stood in the dark. Light from the TV swam over Julia, making it look like she was underwater.

On the table sat a pile of folders, an open laptop and photos. The Watcher could see a picture of hotel room and half of a two-dollar bill on the floor. It meant that Julia had discovered the most important secret. A stiff breeze blew around the side of the house, shaking the shutters. Shivering, the Watcher pulled their coat tighter.

Right now, as she stared at the TV screen, what was Julia thinking?

A voice, carried on the wind, whispered, *You have to find out what she knows.*

His whispered reply, *But how?*

The wind continued to blow, yet there were no answers on the breeze.

The files and computer sat on the table—so close and yet completely out of reach.

Unless…

Over the course of the day, the Watcher had learned everything about Julia McCloud, including her schedule. Dropping the sensor onto the cold ground, the Watcher drove a toe into the white, plastic box until the casing cracked. There was a plan, and nothing would stop them from avenging all the wrongs done to Darcy Owens.

There were fewer than a dozen cars in the entire lot, yet Luis chose a space at the very back. A light above the basement door was the only illumination. He strode across the parking lot, hands in pockets, and wondered if he really needed to attend. He also wondered if every Gamblers Anonymous meeting took place in a church basement.

Pushing open the door with his shoulder, he figured that the answer to both questions was *yes*.

Chairs, gathered in a circle, filled the middle of the room. Most of the seats were filled. The meeting had begun, and a person was speaking, the tone so low that Luis couldn't make out what was being said.

A table, with a coffeepot and a tray of cookies, sat near the wall. Luis filled a foam cup with a dark liquid that resembled coffee, despite the fact that he wasn't thirsty.

Really, he hadn't taken up Liam on the offer to bet on the game, despite the fact that he'd been tempted.

And wasn't it true that families lost touch all the time? It wasn't like Luis and his sister had much in common beyond DNA.

Maybe he didn't need to be at the meeting at all.

He sipped the coffee and knew that something else was true, as well.

If he believed all his excuses, he wouldn't be standing in the basement of a church on a Sunday night. Besides, what had he said to Julia at the firing range?

You won that battle, Julia. From now on, everything else is simple. And as far as help...man. Everyone needs help now and again—even you. I can help you, if you let me.

Luis took an empty seat and stared at his cup of coffee. He needed help, but God, he hated to ask.

He knew the routine. For an hour people spoke. The stories told were all painful, personal and eerily similar. At last, the group leader—an older man with a half moon of hair and an ample middle—stood. A self-adhesive name tag was stuck to his chest. It read Hello, My Name Is Stan. "If nobody else wants to share..."

Luis set his cup of coffee, still almost full, on the floor. "My name is Luis and I really can't remember the last time I was at a meeting. Yesterday, I was having a drink with a buddy. He was talking about his family—his little girl and his girlfriend—and me, I'm single and haven't spoken to my sister in years. We're watching a game on TV and he asks who I think will win. I say Denver because, of course, they'll win. He asks if I want to bet." Luis rubbed his hands up and down the legs of his jeans, wishing he hadn't set down his cup. He needed to do something with his hands. "Anyway, that hunger came back. You know?"

Luis looked up. All eyes were on him and several people nodded their heads.

"I turned down the bet, even though it made me a little sick. My buddy's a good guy. He'd never bring up gambling if he knew about my past, but that's just it. I can't bring myself to tell anyone."

"Why's that?" Stan asked.

"I have another friend. She's great. Pretty. Smart. Tough as nails, but still kind." Luis paused. "I guess she's so close to perfect that I worry if she knew about my addiction, we won't be friends anymore."

"Why's that?"

The answer to that question was hidden deeper in Luis's soul than he cared to look. "I don't know."

"Could you talk to her?" the group leader suggested. "It'd keep you from living in shame."

"I guess," said Luis. "Maybe." *Probably not.*

"Luis, thank you for coming tonight and for sharing."

He picked up the cup from the floor and nodded.

After other people spoke up, the meeting ended. He stood, threw his coffee in the garbage and strode out the door. The cool autumn air revived Luis. He knew that Stan had been right. He'd been living in a cell made out of shame since arriving in Pleasant Pines and the only way to break free was to be honest.

In his career as both a police officer and an operative, Luis had done his fair share of dangerous things—rushing into a burning warehouse, apprehending a serial killer, just to name a few.

Sharing his past with Julia might be the most terrifying thing yet.

He wondered whether he was ready to do it…

Chapter 6

The alarm blared, playing Def Leppard's "Pour Some Sugar on Me." Julia blinked, stretched and sat up. Turning off the alarm, she checked the time—5:30 a.m. The day had yet to break and the world outside was awash in shades of gray. It was Monday morning—the beginning of what promised to be a long week. Yet, if she skipped her run now, she'd pay for it later. After changing quickly into running gear, Julia slipped on a set of earbuds, opened a playlist and strapped her phone to a band on her arm.

Ozzy Osbourne's voice screeched, a moment before the opening chords of "Crazy Train" began. Her blood pulsed with the beat and she stepped out the front door. The street, filled with small single-story houses, was quiet. At this time of the morning, all the houses were dark. A thick coating of frost clung to the dried lawn. After a quick stretch, she took off.

Breath collecting in a frozen cloud, she cleared her mind and ran. Rounding the corner to Main Street, her steps faltered. This morning was the first in a long time she hadn't woken in the grip of a nightmare. So why did she feel like she was in one?

The Watcher sat in the car at the end of the block, hood pulled low. The sheriff emerged from her house. Standing on the porch, she touched her toes, reached overhead and twisted her waist. Seemingly satisfied with her stretch, she jogged down the porch and ran down the street.

From the front seat, the Watcher waited until she disappeared around a corner. Hustling across the street, they climbed the short flight of stairs and opened the front door, stepped inside and pulled it closed.

Pulse hammering, the Watcher stood in the small living room.

What if she came home early?

No. The sheriff was predictable, regimented, disciplined. The Watcher set a timer for thirty minutes—five minutes longer than needed. Seconds ticked off the clock. As the Watcher had seen the night before, the case file sat on the kitchen table. Pictures, fanned out like a deck of cards, filled the counter. Photos of debris from the park. Photos of the body. Pictures from the hotel room, bar and lobby.

There was also a file filled with more than a dozen

witness statements. Many of them referred to seeing the victim with a blond woman. Did the police suspect? What would Darcy do? Then again, they already knew. It was almost as if they share a brain. Using the phone's camera app, the Watcher took pictures of everything. Shoving all the papers back in the file, the Watcher smiled. So far, the plan had worked perfectly.

Now, to the computer. Dropping into the chair, the Watcher opened the lid on the laptop and hit the power button. Ten minutes had already passed.

Yet, there was more than enough time to do what needed to be done and be gone before Julia McCloud ever knew that the Watcher had been here at all.

Peter stared at the monitor, his eyes dry and gritty. Sometime in the middle of the night, he'd wheeled a large dry-erase board into his office. The board was filled with printouts of pictures, along with notes in his cramped handwriting. Taking a sip from his eighth cup of coffee, he stepped back.

He had stumbled upon two stories, not just one.

There was the obvious body discovered in the park. How had the person died? Why hadn't local officials released a statement? Until he had answers, it wouldn't do to print speculation.

Then, there was the mystery of Luis Martinez. He was a former Denver cop, sure, but why had he been given unprecedented access to the scene at the gazebo? And furthermore, why had he left the police force to begin with…and what was he doing in Pleasant Pines?

He'd placed a call to the Denver PD. They had no comment on the subject of Luis Martinez. The weekend PR person wouldn't even confirm Luis's years of employment—facts that were well-documented.

Yet, when Peter asked, "Can you comment on why he left the force after being involved in a case that brought down a Russian drug lord? Shouldn't Detective Martinez have been given a medal or something?" he was shocked by the reply.

"You don't know what you're dealing with. Leave it alone."

Then, the call ended.

The internet provided details of the former cop's life. He wasn't the child star that had come up on the first search. Born in Denver, Luis had been a standout athlete. Despite the talent displayed in high school, he only played two years at a local community college before joining the force. He had one sister, a nurse, who also lived in Denver. The sister had several very active and very public social-media profiles. Each account was filled with family photos. Vacations. Parties. Picnics.

Luis never appeared in any of the pictures.

It was as if Luis didn't exist in his own family.

Why?

That was the question that had kept Peter in the office throughout the previous day. Now, he glanced at the clock on his computer—5:37 a.m.

Hell, he'd been at work all night, too. Honestly, he was too old for this crap. But his journalistic instincts told him there was something going on in his town—and it was his job to figure out what.

Still, he was no closer to answering any of the questions...and he didn't have a story for the paper. Damn it, the past twenty-four hours had been nothing more than a waste of time. Rubbing his eyes, he stood. His knees popped and his shoulder ached. After shuffling across the floor, he filled his empty cup with stale coffee, black as tar.

He sipped and his pulse started to race. It wasn't just the caffeine. His eye was drawn to the bottom of the white board and a four-word notation: Arnie Hatch—in jail.

Arnie Hatch was many things. He was a onetime billionaire. A onetime owner of the Colorado Mustangs, a professional football team that played in Denver. And, currently, Hatch was an inmate in a Colorado state prison. Peter would bet good money that Arnie Hatch would have a thing or two to say about the cop who put him in jail.

Sitting at his computer, he opened a search engine. Within minutes, he had a location for Arnie Hatch and a number for the switchboard at the prison where he was housed. Sure, it was early—still not 6:00 a.m. But Peter had spoken to inmates before. Their days were filled with a whole lot of nothing. As the phone rang, he figured that Hatch would be delighted to speak to a reporter, even at this ungodly hour.

It took only three phone transfers and five minutes to get Hatch on the phone.

"Yeah?" Hatch said, his voice gravelly with sleep.

"Mr. Hatch, my name is Peter Knowles. I'm the editor of the *Pleasant Pines Gazette*—out of Wyoming."

"Yeah, I heard. The guard said when he woke me up. Whaddya want?" Arnie growled.

"I want to ask you some questions about Luis Martinez—he was a detective with the Denver PD."

"I know who Luis Martinez is, the crooked piece of crap."

Peter almost laughed at the hypocrisy. Arnie Hatch had been convicted on several counts—including being a coconspirator for second degree murder, drug trafficking and bank fraud. If he served his entire sentence, Hatch would die in jail. Then again, he still controlled a vast fortune, and with that kind of money, well, you just never knew.

"He's shown up in my town and I'm doing some background research. I'd like to speak to you on the record."

"Sure. Why do you care about Luis Martinez?"

"There's been a death and he's involved in the case."

"Who'd he kill this time?"

"This time?" Peter echoed, his voice sounding shocked even at this hour. "Do you know anything about his relationship with the quarterback who died?"

"He was jealous of his buddy Joe. That was his name. Joe even told me one time that he'd been giving Luis money."

"Money? What for? Cops make okay salaries," Peter said.

"Not if you like to gamble," Arnie replied, and guffawed. "Luis likes to place a friendly bet on games, but he'd gotten into a hole with some disreputable people."

"But I'm sure he had a family to help him out," Peter persisted.

"For a while. But when he got into a hole and was overextended…even his sister stopped talking to him."

Arnie continued, "Twenty K. That's what Luis needed to pay off his debts. Joe, he had that kind of cash. But twenty thousand dollars is a lot of money to a cop."

His voice turned airy. "Joe was a good kid at heart. He got in with the wrong crowd, that's all."

Peter's eyes rolled at the duplicity. Arnie Hatch had been part of the *wrong crowd.*

But he was a fount of information. What a jackpot—no pun intended. "What else do you know about Luis?"

"Not much. I told Joe that if he gave his friend any money, he'd never see it again. Joe, he doesn't care. In fact, he made Luis go to Gamblers Anonymous before giving him any cash. Good kid, Joe."

Peter's stomach started to burn. He wasn't sure if it was all the coffee he'd drank, or if it was the crap that Arnie was trying to feed him about how much he cared for the dead QB.

"Then there were all of those bastards from RMJ."

"RMJ?" Peter echoed.

"Rocky Mountain Justice," said Arnie.

Peter wrote down the words as his foot began to tap. Was it the same agency his news director friend had mentioned? "What do you know about RMJ?"

"Bunch of spooks for hire. One of them, Ian something, a Brit. He was helping Joe's agent. Petra Sloane." Arnie sighed. "And I'm the one in jail. What a world."

Arnie seemed to run out of steam and a long silence stretched out from the other end of the call. "If you think of anything else, get in touch," said Peter, before giving Arnie his number. He then ended the call, his head spinning. He needed some air.

Rising from his desk, he walked through the front office and pulled open the door. Cold air slapped his face, reviving him as he stepped onto the sidewalk. Halfway up the block, the sheriff, red-faced and sweating, ran around the corner.

"Sheriff McCloud," he called out, while lifting a hand and stepping in her way. "I wonder if I could have a word."

Julia slowed to a stop. Hands on her knees, she panted. "Sure. What do you need?"

"I'm Peter Knowles, editor of the *Pleasant Pines Gazette*." He nodded toward the newspaper office. "We met when you first got the job."

"Yeah," she said. "I remember." Standing taller, she wiped her damp face with a sleeve. "What can I do for you?"

He hadn't expected the same bonhomie he'd enjoyed with the late Carl Haak, but Julia's demeanor was about as warm as the chilly morning. Removing his phone from his jacket, he opened the voice recorder. "I'd like to ask you a few questions." He hit Play. "On the record."

"Can you make an appointment or something?"

"Really, this will just take a minute. I was wondering if the sheriff's department had an official statement about the body you took from the park yesterday morning?"

It was all in the eyes, he noted. Julia's eyes got wide for a fraction of a second before narrowing. "Who said anything about a body?"

"Me," he said. "I have eyes. I saw the coroner's van. The body bag. Who was it? What happened?" Peter paused and gave the sheriff a moment of silence to fill. She didn't. He continued, "I spoke to Deputy Cooper, and he said he'd pass on a message."

Julia scratched her brow with her thumb. "Oh, did he?"

"Must've been busy yesterday. Another tourist, dead."

"Who said anything about a tourist? Dead or alive."

Pushing ahead, Peter said, "I spoke to the funeral director yesterday. They weren't called to collect a body. No local funeral means that no local died."

Julia almost smiled. "You're resourceful."

"I am, actually," said Peter, then cleared his throat. Cold air seeped through his thin jacket, leaving him chilled. After blowing on his cupped hands, he continued, "I can help, you know. I grew up in Pleasant Pines. I know everyone. They trust me because I always tell them the truth."

"We're good right now," she said, stepping around him. "But thanks."

And that was it. The new sheriff obviously thought that she was going to shut him out of the story. Well, that was where she was wrong.

He let Julia jog three yards, no more. "Who is Luis Martinez and why is an ex-cop from Denver working on a suspicious death? One so sensitive, your office won't even release a statement."

As if pushed from behind, she stumbled forward. Spinning around, she strode toward Peter with her fists clenched at her side. "Who told you about Luis Martinez?"

"Again, I have eyes. He was with you and Doc in the gazebo." And why had the mere mention of Luis's name set the sheriff on edge?

"No comment," she said with a huff.

"Are you aware that the Denver Police Department let him go?"

"No comment."

"Why would you trust a disgraced cop with a gambling problem, Sheriff?" He held out the phone farther. "And what connection does he have to Pleasant Pines?"

Julia batted the phone from his hand. "I'm done with your freaking questions. You stay out of my investigation, you hear?" She turned on her heel and sprinted away.

Peter's phone was lying on the ground. The screen was cracked, yet the recorder was still running. He replayed the last five seconds. There was a clatter as the phone hit the sidewalk. And then Julia's voice—"I'm done with your freaking questions. You stay out of my investigation, you hear?"—followed by the sound of footfalls on the concrete.

Journalistically speaking, things could have gone better. But as far as having something to print, Peter was in luck. He turned toward the newspaper's office and opened the door. After starting a fresh pot of coffee, he sat back at his desk. Finally, he'd found a story worth telling.

Julia saw nothing but red. She ground her teeth together and muttered every curse word known to humankind. Feet pounding on the pavement, she tried to focus. But there were too many questions jumbled in her mind to think.

How had the reporter found out about Luis? And his history?

And even as she ran, there was one question she couldn't outpace.

Did Luis really have an addiction to gambling? And if he did, why had he never said a word?

She left the downtown business district behind her. Her pulse raced and her side cramped. Long ago, Julia learned to ignore the discomfort and simply breathe. Air went in through the nose, and then, out through the mouth. Once and once more. She raced past streets filled with large homes with wide porches and scrollwork on the eaves. The houses became more modest block by block until she rounded a corner and sprinted up her street. Julia's home was little more than a bungalow. There were two small bedrooms, a half bath in the hallway and a full bath in the master bedroom. Kitchen, dining area and living room all combined to fill a single space.

Her current house was humble when compared to the large mansion she'd grown up in as a child. But she didn't miss the cavernous rooms that were filled with artwork too expensive to touch. Stopping at her front gate, Julia shook her head.

Had she really slapped the phone from the reporter's hand? No, he wasn't simply a reporter—Peter Knowles was the newspaper's editor. Good Lord, she cringed at the possible blowback from her actions.

Then again, the bastard had deserved her enmity. How dare he try to expose Luis. Then she recalled the editor's wide-eyed look of shock. For the first time in months, Julia chuckled to herself and smiled.

The Watcher exhaled before standing. Of course, the computer had been password protected. And despite everything he tried, the device remained locked. It was disappointing, yet inconsequential. Julia kept hard copies of everything. The Watcher had taken pictures of each and every page.

The countdown continued: five minutes, forty-eight seconds remaining.

It was plenty of time to look around.

The Watcher sauntered into the kitchen and opened the cabinets. The food, all healthy, was lined in rows. Cans on the top shelf. Boxes in the middle. Bags on the bottom. The dishes had been washed, dried and put away. The sink was cleaned to the point that it gleamed.

The Watcher's eye was drawn to the hallway and the bedroom beyond. There really wasn't anything to learn about Julia in the neat and tidy kitchen. But the bedroom? That's where the best secrets were kept.

The shades were still drawn, leaving the room dim. Still, the Watcher could see everything—the bed, soft and unmade. The dresser—drawers closed, with photos on the top and arranged in a semicircle. The closet—the door slightly opened, yet everything inside neat and orderly.

In the top drawer of the dresser, there were rows of socks, rolled into balls. Several cotton bras, in shades of black, white and gray, sat next to panties in the same fabric and dull colors.

And yet, at the back of the drawer, there was a flash of red.

It was a thong made of sheer fabric. Running it between finger and thumb, the Watcher wondered when it had last been worn, or if it had been laundered before being put away.

No, that wasn't right. There was the sound of footsteps on the concrete outside. Moving to the window, the Watcher peered through the crack in the drapes. Julia strode up the sidewalk.

Damn it. Now what? There was no way to sneak away without being seen. The Watcher shoved the door closed and stepped into the adjacent bathroom. There was a linen closet, large enough for an adult. After stepping inside, the Watcher pulled the door closed.

Chapter 7

Julia pushed open the front door of her house. After kicking the door closed, she stepped out of her shoes and made her way to her bedroom. What she needed most of all was a shower. After turning the taps on full blast, Julia stripped out of her running gear—leggings and long-sleeved shirt—as steam began to swirl around the room.

She moved to the vanity. For a moment, she studied her own reflection. Blue eyes. Blond hair in need of a trim. Julia had never been a pretty girl—nothing so delicate as that—but she'd grown into an attractive woman. Hadn't she?

Handsome, she'd heard some say, as her reflection disappeared behind a bank of fog. Wiping the mirror clean, she leaned close. There, from the corner of her vision, she saw it and turned.

The linen closet door was ajar.

Julia pushed it closed. But it wouldn't shut. It was stuck on something. The corner of a towel maybe?

She pulled the door.

A person, clad in dark clothes and a hood, lunged toward Julia.

She had no chance to scream. Or fight. Or even think. She was shoved backward, stumbling toward the toilet. She lost her balance and tumbled to the side. Her head connected with the marble vanity and a flash of white filled her vision. On hands and knees, she drew a breath. The pain in her head was like a fire, yet in the distance, she heard footsteps, the slamming of a door. Seconds later, a car engine revved and tires screeched as the vehicle drove away.

Slowly, Julia stood. She held on to the sink as the pain eased. Certain of her footing, she moved back to the bedroom. Her phone sat on the edge of her bed. She opened her contacts and placed the call without a second thought.

Sleep had eluded Luis for most of the night. He'd been lying in bed wondering two things: What would Julia say if she knew about his addiction? And did he have the balls to tell her?

His phone rang and he lifted it from the bedside charger.

"Julia," Luis said, after looking at the caller ID. Maybe now was the time to allow Julia a glimpse of his past—a time when Luis had not been at his best. "I'm glad you called, there's something I've been wanting to tell you."

"Luis," she said. Her voice caught. She inhaled. Exhaled. "There was someone in my house, hiding in my bathroom when I got back from my run."

"What?" He jumped out of bed and stepped into a pair of pants. "Are you hurt?"

"Just a few bruises," she said, her voice shaking.

Then again, Luis knew that not all injuries were physical.

After slipping into a shirt and jacket, he grabbed the keys to his SUV. Running down the stairs, he asked, "Who was it? Did you get a good look at the intruder?"

At street level, Luis sprinted across the sidewalk. Using the fob, he unlocked the doors to his SUV, parked at the curb. Sliding behind the steering wheel, he started the engine and the phone call was transferred via Bluetooth to his in-car stereo system.

"All I saw was a dark hood—pulled so low I couldn't see the eyes. Tufts of long, blond hair. Thin, colorless lips." Julia swallowed. "I know it's impossible, but the person who was hiding in my bathroom…" She paused. "It looked a lot like Darcy Owens."

"What? Can't be. She's in jail." His voice was hoarse, his breathing labored.

"I saw what I saw," she said. "But you're right. Darcy's behind bars. Someone was in my house. Why? What did they want?"

"I'm on your street," said Luis as he approached. "Your block. Your house."

"Come in," said Julia. "The door's unlocked."

He ended the call as he parked the car and sprinted up the walkway. While pushing open the door, he called out, "Julia? It's me."

"Hold on a second," she yelled back. "I need to get dressed." A beat passed. "You can come back."

Luis walked in the door and stopped. Her running gear was lying in a sweaty tangle on the floor. She was clad in the flannel shirt he'd loaned her yesterday. The shirt was big on her, covering her to midthigh. Still, he swallowed as his gaze traveled from her face to her torso to her bare legs. "How are you?" he asked, dragging his eyes away from her legs. "What happened?"

"I was almost in the shower when I found..." Pausing, Julia bit the inside of her lip. "The person hiding." She removed a pair of jeans from her closet and shimmied into the pants, then tied the shirt's hem at her waist.

"Is anything missing?"

"To be honest," said Julia, "I called you first, so aside from putting on clothes, I haven't done much looking. But I walked through the living room. It wasn't like the TV was gone or anything."

"It's probably best to leave everything the way it was," said Luis. He held up his phone. "Mind if I call your deputies and RMJ?"

"Go ahead." While on the phone, Luis looked around her room, taking in every detail. Was anything different? Moved? Gone? The top drawer to her dresser was off-center, the edge no longer flush with the bureau.

Had the intruder been rummaging through her underwear drawer?

"Everyone's on their way," said Luis as he slipped his phone into the pocket of his jeans. "I have to tell you—early morning is an odd time for a home invasion. Your intruder probably isn't a typical burglar."

"I was just starting to think the same thing. Maybe whoever it was knew my schedule. Do you think they knew I'd be out on my morning run?"

Puzzle pieces began to fall into place. And, honestly, Luis didn't like the picture they created.

Julia continued, "Last night, I thought I saw someone looking in the window. But the motion-sensor light was off and when I turned on the porch lights, the yard was empty. And this morning, I cut my run short."

"You cut your run short? Why?"

"I had a run-in with Peter Knowles. He was asking about Tom Dolan, although he doesn't know much, but he had some other questions." Julia sighed, then continued. "Listen, I have to tell you something. It has nothing to do with Tom Dolan, or even the break-in. It looks like Peter Knowles has been doing some digging—"

"Hey," called a voice that Luis knew well. It was Marcus Jones, team leader for RMJ. "You have to come and see what I found."

Whatever Julia had planned to say was temporarily forgotten and Luis followed her to the living area. Marcus stood at the front door, a translucent evidence bag in hand. "I just got here, and I walked the perimeter of your house." He held up the bag, filled with broken bits of white plastic, then entered and closed the door. "This was in the backyard."

Stepping forward, Luis took the bag and examined the contents. "It looks like a motion sensor. It also looks like we know why your light didn't go off last night." He handed the bag back to Marcus.

"Last night?" Marcus echoed. "You need to fill me in on what's happening. I thought this was a simple home invasion."

"At the sheriff's house? You'd have to be the unluckiest criminal in the world to break into a cop's home," said Julia, almost joking. "I'm worried that someone's been watching me."

"I'd say you have more than a reason to worry." Luis gestured to the bag that Marcus held. "Whoever it is, they're bold."

Luis stopped short of giving voice to his greatest fear—that they were more than just bold, but dangerous. The sheriff's office had several open cases—the recent death of Tom Dolan, the disappearance of the leader of the motorcycle club, Christopher Booth, missing for months, and finally, whoever had helped Darcy Owens at the White Winds Resort.

Julia moved to her kitchen. Piles of papers and stacks of files covered the table. There was also a laptop, with the screen up.

"Someone's been on my computer."

"Are you sure?" Marcus asked.

"My mother called, ending a late-night work session. Maybe I was distracted by the call and simply walked away." Julia shook her head. "No, I never leave anything undone."

"Deputy Cooper's on his way," Luis said. "He'll dust it for prints."

"You think whoever's watching me has anything to do with Tom Dolan's death?"

"I'm worried about more than their involvement with the death," said Luis. "I'm worried that someone's been stalking you, and honestly, we have to consider that the killer knows your every move."

Luis watched the color drain from Julia's face. He cursed himself for not having tempered his words. "I'm sorry," he said, his chest tight with regret. "I shouldn't have just blurted out what was on my mind. I mean, we really don't have any proof."

Julia waved away his apology. "You haven't said anything that I haven't thought already." She placed a hand on the back of her head. "It's this damn bruise."

"You hurt your head?" True, Julia had mentioned a few minor injuries when they spoke on the phone. *Damn it.* Luis should've asked about her physical well-being first. "If you have a head injury, you need to get checked out. It could be a concussion."

"I'll be fine—" she began.

"Unless you aren't," Marcus interrupted.

Outside, three vehicles arrived at once. Luis glanced out of the window. It was Wyatt's pickup truck, Liam's silver car and Deputy Cooper's police cruiser. "Looks like the whole crew's here. Let them take care of going through your house for any evidence. I'll take you to the hospital. You need to see Doc Lambert."

Julia glared at Luis. "Like I said—" her jaw was tight "—I'm fine."

"I played football in high school and for two years of community college. Concussions are no joke. I've seen people suffer from headaches for years. Without treatment, sensitivity to light could be severe and long-lasting..."

"I still have to work all day. I need to shower. Eat..."

"Grab your gear. You can get ready at my house and I'll take you to Sally's for breakfast—my treat."

Julia shook her head. "You don't give up, do you?"

Luis smiled. "You know me too well."

There was a knock on the front door. Marcus opened it, and the team—Wyatt, Liam and Travis—entered Julia's house. "Everyone's here," said Marcus. "There's nothing more for you to do, Julia. I'm not your boss anymore, so I can't order you to do anything, but you won't help anyone if you're sidelined."

Julia lifted her hands in surrender. "Fine. Fine. I know when I'm outnumbered. Give me a minute to pack my bag." As she vanished, Luis filled in the team.

Marcus picked up the story, and added, "She thinks they touched her computer."

"And the dresser in her bedroom," said Luis.

"Description?" Liam removed a tablet computer from a leather backpack slung over one shoulder. He opened a screen and began taking notes.

"Well," said Luis, "Julia noted a resemblance to Darcy Owens."

"Just like the woman who was with Tom Dolan in the security video from the inn," said Wyatt.

"Exactly," said Liam. Turning his attention back to the tablet computer, he continued to take notes. The tablet pinged with an incoming message. Liam cursed.

"What is it?" Julia asked. Standing at the end of the short hallway, she was holding a black gym bag. She'd changed out of Luis's shirt. She now had on her uniform—khaki pants, a dark brown shirt and a tin star. It fit her nicely.

"The newspaper published an article about Martinez," said Liam. He scanned the computer screen. "And the sheriff is quoted with a 'no comment.' You spoke to the press about Luis. What the hell, Julia?"

"That wasn't exactly a quote." Julia stepped toward Liam, her nostrils flaring. "The editor ambushed me on my run with a bunch of questions. I didn't comment on anything. In fact, I knocked the phone from his hand and that's why I cut my run short. I wanted to get home and call Luis. But since there was a person in my bathroom who knocked me on my ass, I kinda got sidetracked."

"Okay, you two." Luis stood between Liam and Julia. "We're all on the same team. One story in a local paper isn't anything to worry about," Luis continued, though his chest was tight with concern. RMJ operated in the shadows. In order to do his job, the agency—and the operatives who worked for it—needed anonymity and secrecy. If his name ended up in the press, there'd be no way forward. "I'm still taking Julia to be checked out." He slapped Liam's chest with the back of his hand. "For a head injury, which might've affected her short-term memory or even temporary judgment."

"Point taken," Liam grumbled. "Sorry 'bout what I said, Julia."

"Ain't nothing but a thing. Don't worry."

"Come on." Luis took Julia's bag. "Let's go."

From inside Julia's house, Luis used the fob to start the engine and unlock the doors to his SUV. Without another word, Julia and Luis left her house and walked toward the waiting vehicle. As he slipped into the driver's seat and maneuvered the large vehicle on the small street, Luis couldn't help but wonder—what would happen if his name became public? What would he do if he didn't have RMJ?

At the hospital, Julia was taken into an exam room almost immediately. Doc Lambert had yet to arrive, but Julia was in the capable hands of a nurse practitioner. With nothing but time, Luis found a seat in the empty waiting room and opened the newspaper's app. The headline was brutal. Disgraced Denver Cop Involved in Mysterious Death.

And it got worse.

The story was accompanied by two pictures, both

taken at the gazebo the previous morning. In the first photo, a trio of people—Julia, Doc Lambert and Luis—stood on the stairs while talking. The caption read Sheriff McCloud, Dr. Lambert and Former Denver PD Member Luis Martinez Consult at the Scene of an Unknown Death.

The second photo showed a full body bag being wheeled into the coroner's van. The caption: "Julia McCloud, Sheriff of Pleasant Pines, has no comment on a body that was removed from the town park. Nor does she have a comment on why Luis Martinez, a police officer with a history of gambling addiction and astronomical debts, has been given access to the scene."

Luis set aside his phone and pinched the bridge of his nose. Despite the fact that he was no longer looking at the screen, he could still see the words.

Gambling addiction. Astronomical debts.

Who in the hell was the source for Peter Knowles?

Gambling had ruined Luis's life once. Even though he hadn't placed a bet in more than a year, was it about to ruin his life again?

Julia tapped the toe of her shoe on Luis's boot. "Hey. You look like you're about a million miles away. Everything okay?"

"I should be asking you the same thing. What'd the NP say?"

"Most important, it's not a concussion. Just a bad bump. Ibuprofen if I get a headache." She sat in the seat beside his. "So, what's up?"

The last thing Luis wanted was for Julia to see his flaws. "I checked out the article."

"I'm sorry about what happened with the editor..." she began.

He shoved his phone into her hand. "Just read."

Julia stared at the phone, her eyebrows drawn together. "It's bull, the part about the gambling. I wanted to tell the editor to shove his lying crap. But if I told him that, then it'd be confirming your involvement."

"It's not bull," said Luis. His voice was low, even though no one else was around. "You know I was friends with the QB who died, right?"

"Joe," said Julia. "I remember."

"We grew up together, kind of like brothers." Luis dropped his gaze and stared at the floor as he spoke. He knew he could stop the story now. Julia would never press him to say more. Then again, if he didn't speak now, would he ever? "Joe was a wonder kid on the field. I was good, sure. But Joe, well, he was great."

Julia placed her hand on his shoulder. "It's okay. Whatever happened, it's in the past and it'll be okay."

He wanted to believe her. But nothing had been okay—not since the first time he placed a bet. "It was my first year of community college. Joe, he was at a big university. I was talking smack with one of my teammates who was saying that Joe wasn't the real deal. Joe was my boy, so I had to put down a Benjamin to protect his honor. It was against the rules to wager on games, but only if we got caught. And then

I won. The feeling…aww, man. It was like my first kiss, sex and giving a glass of water to a man who was dying of thirst, all at the same time."

"So what the reporter said wasn't bull?" Julia asked, her palm still on his shoulder.

He brushed her fingertips with his own. God, it felt good to touch her hand. "I kept chasing that high. You win some, you lose some. But I never had a rush like the first time. And then, I quit winning and it was only lose, lose, lose." He cleared his throat. "I lost everything. Borrowed so much money from my family that my own sister wouldn't take my calls, even now. Joe was my last resort to pay off some serious loan sharks. He gave me the cash, but I had to go to Gamblers Anonymous. At the second meeting I figured out what I needed to do to stay clean. That was the day he died." Luis's throat was dry. He coughed. "I never got a chance to thank him."

"He knows," said Julia. "Somehow, he does."

"You really believe that?" Luis asked, his fingers still twined through hers. "I never took you for a religious type."

"In this life." Still holding his hand, she stood and pulled Luis to his feet. "You have to have faith that things will work out in the end. Otherwise, there's no point to what we do."

They stood facing each other, so close that he could feel the whisper of her breath on his chest. He still held her hand. All he needed to do was pull her closer, and then she'd be in his arms.

Is that what he wanted? And what about her?

How much would one kiss ruin their friendship and comradery?

Julia cleared her throat and stepped back. “Come on, let’s get to work. It’s late already.”

A wall clock gave the time as 7:25 a.m. Most mornings, Luis would still be in bed.

With a shake of his head, Luis remained where he stood. “You should call Wyatt and get him to partner with you. If I stay on the case, I’ll just be a distraction.”

“To who? Me? Forget what the newspaper published and let’s go.” She let her hand slip from his. “And thanks for trusting me with your confession. For the record, your past doesn’t matter to me. But I appreciate your honesty now.”

She walked away, leaving Luis with a choice to make. Did he follow? Or did he give up on the case, on RMJ, on Julia? No, the job with RMJ had saved his life. He owed the agency everything. And Julia?

Well, how he felt about her was a bit more complicated…and those feelings, he decided, were best ignored.

Chapter 8

Julia showered at Luis's apartment. While she was getting ready, he'd picked up breakfast from the local diner, Sally's on Main. They ate quickly, and soon they were walking down the stairs of his third-floor apartment to a private door on the street level.

On the landing, Luis opened the door and held it as Julia passed. Slipping on her aviator sunglasses, despite the gray skies, she gave him a quick smile. "Always the gentleman."

"Always," he agreed while pulling the door shut. He turned the handle to make sure that the lock had engaged. It had. "You know, you're welcome to stay at my place for a night or two. If you'd be more comfortable after the break-in, I mean."

What struck Julia was not that Luis had offered

his apartment as a place to crash, but the carnal images that filled her mind. Tongues. Mouths. Flesh. Sweat. Julia swayed as she walked. Then again, he'd only made the offer to be nice and there was nothing more she should be reading in to the suggestion.

She cleared her mind of every indecency and continued to walk, planning her day and prioritizing items with each step. "Finding out what happened to Tom Dolan is at the top of the list," she said.

"You don't think he was killed? Doesn't finding half of a two-dollar bill prove that he was murdered, and somehow, the new killer is linked to Darcy Owens?"

"I think I want to see the toxicology reports." She turned to Luis. "Any update from Chloe?"

Luis glanced at his phone. "Not yet."

Julia walked on, lost in her own thoughts.

Pleasant Pines looked much as it had when the town had been cut out of the wilderness in the late 1800s as a railroad hub for the silver mines. The buildings were pure Victorian architecture—tall and narrow—and many were made of brick or stone. The original scrollwork on the eaves of homes was impressive to Julia, and she'd seen a fair share of fine houses in her lifetime.

The sheriff's office was located in the county office building, a structure that dated to the town's founding, and filled one quarter of the second floor. It consisted of two rooms. The larger room of the two served as a squad room/reception area. One wall was filled with tall windows that overlooked the town park and gazebo.

A set of chairs along the adjacent wall served as a waiting area. Rose, the office manager, had a desk at the back of the room. Tucked behind Rose's desk was another door, and that one led to Julia's personal office.

Opening the door, Julia entered the squad room and her pace slowed. Luis was right behind her. A man, early thirties by her guess, sat in one of the chairs at the back of the room. He looked familiar, yet Julia couldn't remember where she'd seen him, or even who he was.

Rose sat behind her desk. "You have a visitor, Sheriff. And before you go back to your office, Mr. Taylor called again. He says that someone's in the woods by his house. You want me to send a deputy to talk to him?"

Mr. Taylor, retired from the Marine Corps, lived outside of town. Since his wife died a few years back, he'd had nobody to keep him company except an old dog. The sheriff's department made regular wellness checks. It seemed like now was the time to make another visit. Julia had already put a lot of responsibility on her staff. She couldn't ask for much more. "I'll get in touch with Mr. Taylor." Although, she had no idea when…

"I worry about Mr. Taylor out there all alone," said Rose. "I have some cookies. Will you drop them off when you go?"

"Sure thing," said Julia. Then, turning to the

visitor, she continued, "I'm Sheriff McCloud. You wanted to speak to me?"

"I recognized you. From the newspaper, I mean." The man stood. "Robert Carpenter," he said, holding out a business card.

Julia took the offered card. Robert E. Carpenter was the general manager of an auto-parts store located in a town ninety miles from Pleasant Pines. She wasn't in the mood to be sidetracked. Since all the desks were empty, she assumed that the two deputies were on patrol…meaning that she couldn't ask one of them to take a statement. Still, Julia knew a lot of responsibilities came with her job, and not all of them had anything to do with investigating what had happened to Tom Dolan. "You've made quite the trip, Mr. Carpenter. What can I do for you?"

"Call me Robert," he said. "I went to high school with Darcy Owens. I just read the article about the newest guy being found in the gazebo. I have some information that might be useful. Since I was in town, I thought I should stop by."

Julia stood taller. Now she remembered—Robert Carpenter was the former desk manager at the White Winds Resort, the same place where Darcy Owens hid while escaping justice. There was a connection between Carpenter and Owens by way of the high school they both attended. Yet, Carpenter hadn't been at work on the day Darcy contacted the resort, giving him an alibi.

So far, nobody had been charged as an accessory

or coconspirator for the crimes committed by Darcy Owens. It was something Julia intended to change.

"Come with me," she said.

Holding open her office door for Robert and Luis, Julia waited as the men crossed the threshold. "Have a seat," she said, before sliding into the big leather chair that sat behind the desk.

Luis closed the door and then leaned against the wall. He asked, "How well did you know Darcy?"

Dropping into a chair opposite the desk, Robert sighed. "She was my girlfriend. We dated my entire senior year. She was only a sophomore, but we grew up near each other. My house is on the other side of the woods from hers, so I guess you can say that I knew her as well as anyone can know someone else."

"What did you know about her home life? Her parents?"

Robert scratched his cheek. "If you're asking me if she was abused by her father, the answer is yes. She confided in me when we got serious."

It was exactly what Julia wanted to know. Reaching for a pad of paper and a pen, Julia began to take notes. "You said you had information about Darcy Owens? What is that?"

Robert leaned back in his seat and rubbed his chin. "Darcy has this cousin, Bethany Edwards. They're the same age and look almost identical, or they did back in high school. Anyway, when they were kids, Bethany would do stuff and then later blame Darcy."

Forced to use her left hand, Julia's penmanship

was horrible. Her palm cramped as she held tight to the pen. Robert stopped and Julia stretched her fingers.

Luis asked, “What kind of stuff?”

“I remember once in middle school Bethany stole a girl’s lunch and put it in Darcy’s locker. We all kind of thought it was funny, even though we knew it was mean.”

Hilarious, thought Julia. But not equal to the crimes Darcy committed. “Anything else?”

Robert paused. He rubbed his chin again. “I think in a lot of ways Bethany was jealous of her cousin. Right before the homecoming dance, Bethany was supposed to give Darcy a trim, but she cut off all her hair. She sheared off part of her scalp, too. It was a bloody mess. Darcy couldn’t go to the dance, and her parents never let me come over. So…”

“So what happened?”

“I ended up taking Bethany.”

Julia didn’t want to feel bad for Darcy Owens, truly she didn’t. Yet, she couldn’t help herself when she said, “That must’ve sucked for her.”

“Yeah, I guess it did.”

“Anything else?” Julia asked.

“Actually, yeah,” he said.

Julia let silence settle in the room and waited for Robert to fill it.

Finally, he said, “The things that Darcy’s dad did to her.”

“The abuse?”

“Yeah. Well, he did that to Bethany sometimes,

too." Robert paused again. "That night at the homecoming dance, Bethany told me that she blamed Darcy for the abuse and was eventually going to make her pay."

Robert Carpenter left and let the door close behind him. Luis stood in Julia's office, and adrenaline raced through his system. Undoubtedly, Robert Carpenter had just provided a reasonable suspect in the killing of Tom Dolan—Darcy's cousin, Bethany Edwards. Never mind that Julia was reluctant to call the death a murder until the tox reports came back. The dude had been whacked.

"We have to do some snooping into Bethany Edwards's internet footprint and see what we can find."

"Sure thing," said Julia. She hit the power button on her computer.

"Oh, no," he said. "We're going to RMJ's office and use the good stuff."

Julia smiled in return. "I'm in."

Taking Julia's official vehicle, an ancient pickup truck, they drove from the county office building to RMJ's headquarters. To the untrained eye, it appeared to be any other well-maintained property.

Yet, to those who knew enough to look, it was so much more.

As Julia pulled up at the corner, Luis knew they'd been caught by one of more than a dozen cameras that surrounded the property. As they strode up the walk, the lock clicked as they approached the door. He turned the handle and they stepped inside.

Every time he came to work, Luis felt as if he was living inside a spy flick.

Marcus stood on the threshold. "I saw you two driving up the street," he said.

Luis let Julia go first, then he said, "We need to do some internet searching."

"Let's get you started," said Marcus.

The most powerful computers were located on the second floor, at the end of the hallway, in a climate-controlled room.

"What are you looking for?" Marcus asked.

"We found an interesting lead. It seems as if Darcy Owens has a cousin who could be her twin," said Julia, settling into a seat.

"Really? That fits with the person you saw in your house, right? And the woman who was caught on camera."

She nodded. "It does."

Luis turned his attention to the wall of computer monitors. Within minutes, they knew all there was to know about Bethany Edwards from her public social media accounts. Age. Address. Along with the fact that she'd recently gotten a divorce. They even had her car's make, model and license plate from a picture that she'd posted.

"She's a divorced mom with two children," Julia said as she read from the screen. "A boy and girl. It looks like she took back her maiden name after the divorce and works as a dental hygienist."

Bethany had also pinned dozens of recipes on a

board entitled Healthy Recipes That Kids Will Actually Eat.

She chatted online with a group of women about educational TV. And she belonged to another group that discussed dating after a divorce. It was all as Luis expected to find, except for one thing.

"She does a lot of searches for Darcy Owens," said Luis, scrolling through her internet history that the wizards at RMJ were able to find.

"Do you begrudge Bethany her curiosity? After all, they're cousins." Julia leaned her elbow on the table. She was putting up a strong front, but Luis could tell—by the paleness of her skin and the dark circles around her eyes—that Julia was exhausted. More than that, someone had actually been in her home, violated her privacy.

"How're you doing? This morning was intense."

She touched the back of her head. "The bump doesn't hurt at all."

"You can take the day off, Julia. Nobody'd blame you if you did."

"I took off enough time after what happened with the damn hand and my gut." She shook her head. "Besides, we have to find out what happened to Tom Dolan. He deserves justice and the town deserves peace. I'm not going to let a bruise and a startle stop me from doing my job."

"Fair enough," he said.

Holding a tablet computer, Wyatt appeared at the door. "Marcus said you two were here." He sat down and held out the computer. "I was going through the

Darcy Owens file last night and I have a theory about our current killer."

"You do?" Julia leaned forward. "What is it?"

"It's simple, really. There were two things Darcy did with each of her victims. First, she left half of a ripped two-dollar bill in their wallet. But she also took a trophy. I looked at the pattern with all her suspected killings." Wyatt held up the computer. A man's face, along with a name filled the screen. "This is Sven, her third victim. He had the half bill in his wallet, just nothing taken from his person. It's the same with the first two victims."

"Just to clarify," Julia began, "you're saying that Darcy taking tokens from her victims evolved over time?"

"Killing is like any other skill. The more murders you commit, the better you get. You finesse your methods. Maybe there was something the fourth victim had that Darcy wanted. She took it and her MO changed. But, with the most recent victim, Tom Dolan, nothing was taken. His brother-in-law, Sean, accounted for all his belongings."

"It's interesting," Luis admitted. "How can that help us find out what happened to Tom?"

"We all agree that this isn't a simple copycat killer," said Wyatt. As if a copycat killer would be simple to begin with. "The killer knows about the two-dollar bill, but not the trophy-taking. If they're replicating Darcy's crimes, it's from a time that was early in her development."

"So it's someone from her past," said Julia. "Like, maybe a cousin."

"Exactly," said Wyatt.

"Then let's see if we can find any evidence linking Darcy's cousin to the Pleasant Pines Inn on Saturday night." Luis returned to the computer before maneuvering through the internet to the DMV's site.

"What're you doing?" Julia asked.

"Checking out if Bethany's car went through one of a dozen traffic lights on Saturday night—her plates would have been read and recorded."

"Poking around on her social media is one thing. Can you do this without a warrant?"

"*You* can't," he said, "but I can. Working for RMJ gives me..." He paused, looking for the right word. "Latitude."

Julia huffed, but she knew he was right. "If this case ever goes to trial..."

"We'll get you the correct warrant before you ever produce the evidence," Luis said.

"I don't like it."

He'd been a cop. He knew how laws worked. "Do I search or not?"

Julia opened and closed her injured hand. "Go ahead, but just this once."

Luis entered the information for Bethany Edwards's car, then set the parameters for Saturday evening through Sunday morning and waited.

Within minutes, a list appeared. No photos.

Beginning at 10:00 p.m., Bethany Edwards had

driven from her home to the Pleasant Pines Inn. She stayed for ninety minutes before returning home.

"The timing is perfect to make her the woman in the video with Tom Dolan," said Julia.

Which meant one thing: Bethany Edwards was certainly their prime suspect.

Chapter 9

"We have to talk to Bethany," said Luis. "She matches the description of the person on the video and the person who broke into your house, Julia. She reads about the cases obsessively. She's a relative of Darcy's and might know how half of a two-dollar bill is placed with each of the victims. Plus, according to Robert Carpenter, Bethany was also abused by Darcy's father."

Julia looked at Bethany's address. She lived in an apartment in a town to the east of Pleasant Pines. "Let's go and talk to her, then. But first, I want to make a stop. There's an elderly man who lives by himself and called because he thinks someone is in the woods near his house. With everything going on, I want to drop by and make sure he's okay."

Since the old man's house was between Pleasant Pines and the home of Bethany Edwards, Julia decided to stop by and visit the retired vet first. Luis, riding shotgun, agreed to the detour.

In Pleasant Pines, Mr. Taylor was known by many names, including Sergeant Taylor and Sarge. He'd served in the US Marine Corps during the Korean War and now lived in a rambling old house at the end of a dirt road. The Sarge's wife died more than twenty years ago. His kids were all grown and lived in other parts of the state. It left the older man with nobody to keep him company other than a tick hound named Gunner and a few scrawny chickens.

"You'll like the Sarge," she said as she pulled off the paved road.

"I'll like him," Luis stated, echoing her words. "Why's that?"

She gave Luis a sidelong glance. "You'll see."

The house, a two-story wooden structure, sat in the middle of a wide lawn. An American flag hung from a flagpole and fluttered in the morning breeze. A long porch stretched across the front of the house. As Julia parked the truck, a brown-and-black dog charged across the grass. The dog pawed at the door, his tail a wagging blur.

Julia jumped down from the truck and the dog began to bellow. The front door opened. Sergeant Taylor, wearing an olive-drab T-shirt and jeans, stepped onto the porch.

"Well, if it isn't my favorite army officer turned

police officer," he said, his smile wide. "Come in. I just started a pot of coffee. You can help me drink it."

Julia grabbed the bag from the truck. "Rose sent over some cookies. And I brought a friend. Luis Martinez."

Luis stepped to the ground.

"Well, the cookies will go nice with the coffee, and Luis, you are always welcome here, 'cept that means there's less coffee and cookies for us, Sheriff McCloud." He held open the front door. "Come in, come in." The dog bounded up the steps and ran into the house. "You, too, Gunner," he said, laughing at the dog.

The lights were off in the small sitting room, yet it wasn't so dark that Julia couldn't see the walls. They were covered with pictures of military service, citations and awards. In short, Sarge's living room was a timeline of duty and honor. Seeing the photos filled Julia with a sense of awe.

The kitchen, floor covered in yellow linoleum, was at the back of the house. A small TV sat on the counter. The screen was filled with a morning newscast with the sound muted. Sarge gestured to a round, wooden table. "Have a seat. And, Luis, tell me the two most important things about a man."

Luis dropped into a chair, a small smile on his face. "What's that, sir?"

"Sir," Sarge echoed. "I like this young man, Julia. He's a keeper." Inhaling, he turned back to Luis. "Have you ever served in the military and how do you take your coffee?"

"I have never had the privilege of serving in the military," said Luis. "And I take my coffee black."

"Luis is a retired police officer from Denver. He's consulting on a case," Julia added.

Sarge poured three cups of coffee and passed them all around before putting the cookies on a plate. "The case you're consulting on," said Sarge, as he sat. "Is it about whoever's living in the woods behind my house?" He lifted a cookie from the plate, then held it out to Gunner. The dog ate the treat in one bite.

"Rose didn't say anything about someone living on your property, just that you thought someone had trespassed."

"I don't want to frighten Rose, now, do I? I didn't mention that there was a blanket missing from the back of my car, or that I'm short by one box of cereal because she'd be scared for me. Plus, the last few nights, I've smelled a campfire."

Julia sipped her coffee. When she'd first met the older man, she found him charming, energetic and possibly too old to live alone, especially since his house was so far from any family or neighbors. She worried that too soon he'd have to change his living arrangement—either move into town, or better yet, stay with a relative. Was now the time? Still, it was Julia's job to check out his claims. And if the blanket was misplaced and the box of cereal eaten and then forgotten, she'd have something to share with Sarge's grown children.

She asked, "Do you know approximately where you smelled the campfire?"

"There's a trail that runs through the woods. I'd guess it was about a quarter of a mile back. Far enough away that I couldn't see the light but could smell the smoke."

Julia sipped her coffee again. "When was the last time you talked to your son? The one who lives in Casper?"

"I spoke to both of my boys last week." Sarge slipped the dog another cookie. "I know what you're getting at. Carl Haak thought I was too old be living alone in the middle of the woods, too. And sure, I can't go through the night without taking a leak. Doc Lambert has me taking pills for high blood pressure and such, but I'm still together up here." He tapped his temple. "That's what counts."

"You're right, Julia," said Luis, a cookie in hand. "I do like Sergeant Taylor."

Julia's face flamed red and hot. "I hadn't meant to imply—" she began.

"Sure you did." Sarge waved away her comment. "But I forgive you. After all, you can't expect much from someone from the army." He winked to show he was teasing.

After taking a final sip of coffee, Julia rose from the table. "Let me go look for that campfire and I'll tell you know what I find."

Luis got to his feet, too.

"I appreciate you coming out here to check on an old man…and for your concern," said Sarge as he walked them to the front door. "You see that trail? Right between those two big trees?"

"I do, indeed," Julia said with a wave as she and Luis headed out.

Less than fifty yards onto the trail, the woods pressed in on either side, and she'd lost sight of the house.

"You know what I want to be when I grow up?" Luis asked. He shoved the last bite of cookie into his mouth. "That guy."

"Told you that you'd like him."

"You think he's confused about all the stuff missing from his house?"

Julia shrugged. "Could be, but we won't know until we check it out."

The trail followed the terrain and crested a rise. There, on the other side of the ridge, was a blackened pile of wood. "Looks like the campfire part of his story checks out." Luis approached the charred logs and held out his hand. "It's cold, but look at this." He held up a burned piece of cardboard. Despite the fact that the edges were blackened and brittle, the words *full of fiber* were clear.

"Looks like his cereal really was missing, too," said Julia. She turned in a slow circle. "But I don't see a blanket."

"You think it's someone living rough? A transient, maybe."

"Maybe."

Sun shining through the branches glinted off

something metallic. "What's that?" Julia asked, traipsing through the underbrush.

There, atop a pile of leaves, was a metal badge. She lifted it from the ground. The wording was unmistakable. The Transgressors. They were a local motorcycle club. Several members had been arrested for drug trafficking and prostitution last year. The leader, Christopher Booth, had escaped during the raid and was still at-large. "Look at this." She held up the insignia.

"You think it belongs to Booth?"

"I do," said Julia. "Which means that the Sarge was right. And he isn't safe out here by himself."

Julia retraced her steps, ever vigilant for a sign that Christopher Booth was watching. When they got back to the house, Sarge was sitting in a rocker on the porch, a cup of coffee in his hand.

"You find anything?"

"We did. It looks like someone's been living on your property and has become audacious enough to break into your house. I want to have my deputies patrol this area, but until we catch the culprit, I'd like you to stay with one of your sons. Or another friend. Or relative."

"If someone's living in the woods, and they need help," said Sarge, "they don't have to steal from me. I'll invite them in. Give 'em food. A place to stay."

"This guy isn't just down on his luck," said Luis. "He's actually bad news. You remember anything about the motorcycle club arrested a few months back?"

"The one that held all those young women against their will, you mean?" asked Sarge.

"That's the one. Julia found a badge near the campsite. My worry—her worry—is that it belongs to one of those criminals. For now, you aren't safe."

"Can I call your son for you?" Julia asked.

"Don't bother. I'll go stay with Sally for a few days."

"Sally?" Luis echoed. "Like from the restaurant?"

"She and I go out every now and again," said Sarge. "The woman can cook. Second best pie in the world—after my dearly departed wife, that is."

"You promise that you're going to go?" Julia asked. "Do you want us to help you pack?"

"I've got stuff of mine at her place," said Sarge. "I'll lock up and then Gunner and I will be off."

It took the older man only minutes to secure his house. Then the dog climbed into the front seat of a 1977 Cadillac DeVille. With the smell of exhaust trailing behind, they drove away.

"Let's go," said Julia. It was nearly 10:30 a.m. and they hadn't even spoken to Bethany Edwards. Starting the engine, Julia was ready to question the sole suspect in the murder of Tom Dolan.

Luis slid into the passenger seat and slammed the door closed. "The Sarge is a trip, that's for sure. Sally can cook? Second best pie? What'd you think?" he asked. "Is the old guy talking about dessert or not?"

"Don't even start," said Julia, putting the gearshift into Drive. "Don't even start."

* * *

The apartment complex where Bethany Edwards lived consisted of a dozen buildings that surrounded a central playground. Several preschool-aged children and toddlers ran around the swing sets or climbed on the play structure. Mothers stood nearby in tightly knit groups, watching the children and chatting.

"It looks like the buildings are lettered. *A* through *L*. Two apartments in front. Two in the back. Three stories. If Bethany Edwards lives in E-12, she'd be in this building," said Luis as Julia eased the large truck into a parking space designated for visitors.

Julia was hardly listening. In fact, she was barely able to draw in a breath. She stared out the window as her stomach began to churn. A blond woman wearing a pink jacket stood in the middle of a group. A small, towheaded boy launched himself into the woman's arms. She swung him in a wide circle before pulling him in for a hug and kiss.

It was her—the woman from the bunker. The same one from her house, too.

And yet, not.

"There she is," said Julia, pointing. Realizing that her finger was trembling, she lowered her hand and gripped the steering wheel tighter.

Luis glanced out the widow. "Looks like that's our suspect, all right."

The group of mothers watched as Julia approached the playground, with Luis by her side. She made eye contact with Bethany Edwards. The woman still held her son. "I'm Sheriff McCloud from Pleasant Pines—are you Bethany Edwards?"

"I am."

"I have a few questions for you."

"About?"

"Your cousin. Darcy Owens."

Bethany's cheeks turned pale. She kissed her boy on the head. While handing him to another one of the ladies, she asked, "Can you keep an eye on my kids for a few minutes?"

"Sure thing," said the friend.

Then to Julia, Bethany said, "Let's go inside."

Julia nodded and followed as Bethany led them to her apartment and opened the door. Curtains had been pulled across a sliding glass door, and beyond was a small porch. The interior was cool and dim. The air smelled distinctly of baby shampoo and chocolate chip cookies. Colorful blocks and books littered the floor and a pile of laundry sat, folded, on the kitchen table. Pictures of two children—happy and smiling—lined the walls.

Without question, Julia was having a hard time placing Bethany Edwards as the person she'd seen at her house this morning.

"Have a seat," said Bethany, gesturing to a striped sofa.

Julia sat. Luis remained on his feet.

Bethany sank into a rocking chair. "I have to be honest," she said. "I was wondering why it took you so long to find me."

* * *

Luis didn't waste time with niceties. "Where were you Saturday night and early Sunday morning?"

"Home," said Bethany. "Here."

"Anyone to verify that fact?" Julia asked.

"I had a date who stopped by after I put my kids to bed. He was here from about nine o'clock until eleven."

"Can I get a name and number for your date?" Julia asked.

"Of course." She got up and ripped a corner from a piece of paper. After scrawling both her date's name and phone number on the scrap of paper, she handed it to Julia and returned to her seat.

"What about your car?" After all, they had reports that a car, registered to Bethany Edwards, had driven from her apartment to the Pleasant Pines Inn and back.

"My car," Bethany echoed. She continued, "You said this is about Darcy?"

"Can you answer the question?" Julia asked.

"Sure, I loaned my car to a neighbor. She had a GNO planned and was the designated driver. She didn't want to let her friends down, so I offered my ride."

"GNO?" Luis asked.

"Girls' night out," said Julia. "What's your friend's name and address?"

"Candace Johnson," said Bethany. Pointing to the door, she said, "She lives directly across from me."

Until they'd spoken to the neighbor, there was nothing more to ask about the car being on the road. Leaning his shoulder on the wall, Luis asked, "How would you characterize your relationship with your cousin?"

"I haven't spoken to Darcy in years. Not since her mom died." Bethany chewed on her bottom lip. The woman was uncomfortable. True, speaking to the police often left people jittery. But was there more?

"You know she's in jail, though," said Julia.

"Sure. Her story's kind of hard to miss. It's been in the paper and on TV. I've even seen her mentioned on the national news."

"Would you say that you follow her story closely?" Julia asked.

She shrugged.

"You haven't visited her? Called?" According to the reports, Darcy had had no visitors, calls or correspondence, other than her attorney.

Bethany shook her head. "No."

"How close were you and Darcy as kids?" Julia asked. "Did you spend much time at her house?"

"Not really. My mother didn't like her father. She said he was a creep. We went to school together but didn't socialize much." She paused a beat and added, "I feel guilty about what happened to her, what she became."

"Why is that?" Julia asked.

Bethany's voice was low. "Her father abused me once. I knew what he did to her and I never told a teacher or anything. My parents knew but they were only worried about me."

"Did you help Darcy Owens kill her parents?" Luis asked.

"No," said Bethany. "I'll admit that I wasn't upset

when Uncle Frank turned up dead, but my parents cut off all ties with her family after what happened to me."

That didn't fit with the information provided by Robert Carpenter. Yet, Luis knew there was a very thin line to be walked while questioning Bethany Edwards. Right now, she was cooperating. He also knew that she could stop at any moment—or worse, ask for a lawyer. "What about at school?"

"What about it?" Bethany asked.

"You and Darcy attended the same high school. You were even in the same grade. You never spoke to her in class?"

"If we had a class, I spoke to her, but we weren't friends. Darcy wasn't really close to anybody at school."

"What about Robert Carpenter?"

"Who?" Bethany asked.

"Your date to homecoming after you gave Darcy a haircut that left her head bloody."

"I never." She drew her eyebrows together and looked around the room as if an answer was somehow hidden in a corner. "I don't even know what you're talking about." Bethany stood. "I've left my kids for too long. I need to get back outside."

Julia stood, too. Like him, she knew that the interview was over. Bethany opened the front door and waited for them to exit. She followed, closing the door behind her. They stood in the breezeway as Bethany walked down the steps without a backward glance.

Chapter 10

They remained on the stoop between Bethany's apartment and the one belonging to her neighbor, Candace Johnson. Luis lifted his hand and knocked.

"Hold on," a woman called out.

A moment later, the door opened. Julia held up her badge. "Candace Johnson? I'm Sheriff McCloud from Pleasant Pines. This is my colleague, Luis Martinez. We have some questions."

The woman, in her midtwenties with short brown hair and a snake tattoo wrapped around her wrist, stepped back. "Questions? What's this all about?"

"We need to know your whereabouts on Saturday evening between ten o'clock and half-past twelve."

"That's easy," she said. "I was out with friends—

actually, at the pub in the Pleasant Pines Inn. Is everything okay?"

"Can you tell us how you got there?" Julia asked.

"I drove," said Candace. "But I borrowed a friend's car. Mine's in the shop."

"Does your friend have a name?"

"Bethany Edwards." Candace pointed to the door across the landing. "She lives right there."

Julia removed a pad of paper and pen from her pocket and held them out to Candace. "Can you give us the names and numbers for the friends you were with on Saturday?"

She took the paper and pen. "Sure," she said while writing. "Here you go." She handed the pad and pen back to Julia.

"One more thing before we let you go," said Luis. "Any idea where Bethany was while you were out?"

"She had a date stopping by after the kids went to bed. That's why she didn't need the car. Then again, she really doesn't go out that often."

Julia tucked the notepad back into her pocket. "Thanks for your time."

With Luis at her side, Julia turned for the stairs. Once they were back in the parking lot, Julia cursed. "Well, that was a complete dead end."

"Not necessarily," said Luis, rounding to the passenger side of the truck.

"How can you say that? Bethany not only has an alibi—she was home with her kids—but she was also without a ride. Still…" She pulled open the door and slipped behind the steering wheel. "I'll contact the people Candace listed and maybe we can get another look at the hotel video."

"I don't think there are many more answers on the video than those we've already gotten," said Luis. "It's like what Wyatt said. Whoever killed Tom Dolan knows Darcy well, and probably during her formative years. Her ex-boyfriend and her cousin are likely candidates to know all her secrets."

"I agree, but how do we figure out which one? We should talk to Robert Carpenter again, don't you think?"

Luis nodded. "There's something I'd like to do first, though."

"Yeah, what's that?"

"We have to go where it all started." Luis paused. "We have to go to Darcy's childhood home."

Julia knew Luis was right. They'd have to visit the place where Darcy grew up…and her need for murderous vengeance was born.

Luis sat in the passenger seat as Julia steered the big truck out of the apartment complex. If the GPS was right, the trip would take less than two hours.

The drive passed in complete silence. For Luis, it was a chasm he didn't know how to cross. And Julia seemed focused on the road and her thoughts. Finally, as they pulled off the main road and onto the gravel drive, the sun started to peek through cracks in the cloud cover. Beams of light slanted down on the woods that surrounded the property.

The truck crested a small rise and the house came

into view. It was a white two-story home with a sagging porch and shutters that hung askew. Otherwise, the structure looked to be intact. But he couldn't help but wonder how many secrets the house held.

Luis had been at the hospital with Julia when Darcy Owens had been apprehended at this very same home. All the same, he'd been briefed about the episode and recalled the details.

"The second story consists of four rooms and a bath. I say we start with Darcy's bedroom. It's been searched already, but you never know what we might find. Besides, it's probably best to start at square one."

Julia nodded. "Okay," she said.

They exited the car and strode to the front door. The boards of the porch sagged and groaned with each step. It had been months since the home had been searched and the remnants of crime-scene tape, like tattered flags, hung limply from the porch. A lockbox with a ten-digit code had been attached to the front door. Inside was a key to the front door.

Julia had the code and unlocked the door. Luis pushed it open. Rusty hinges squeaked and dust motes, disturbed by the movement, rose and swirled in a frenzied dance. The air was stale and smelled faintly of mold.

They entered a front room, complete with a crumbling fireplace and a sofa that vomited stuffing. The floor was covered with a ripped and stained carpet. Wallpaper hung in strips and chunks of plaster had fallen from the ceiling. Straight back and to the right, a set of stairs led to the second floor.

Despite the decay and neglect, Luis could tell that something was wrong with the house. Without question, he knew that something bad had happened here. It was as if the walls and floors, and even the foundation, had absorbed the negative energy.

Luis held a wobbly balustrade and placed his foot on the first step. Pressing down, he bounced a little. The step held. The next step was solid, as was the one after that. With only half a dozen stairs left, Luis heard a crack. His shin filled with fire and his foot dropped away. "What the…?"

He looked down but knew what he would see. He'd broken through the rotten wood of the step. The sharp edges of wood had ripped the fabric of his jeans and sliced open his flesh. Hot blood trickled down his leg, filling his shoe. Pulling his leg free, he cursed.

"We need to get you back down to the truck," said Julia. "There's a first-aid kit in there."

"I don't need a first-aid kit," he said. "I'm tough. I can handle the pain."

"There's rodent droppings all over the place and it reeks of mold in here. Nobody is tough enough to fend off all these germs if they get in an open wound. When was the last time you had a tetanus shot?"

He grimaced. "Two, maybe three years ago."

"You should be good then." Julia hooked her arm under his shoulder, drawing him close. God, she smelled so good—and holding her felt better. "You want to go up or down?"

Luis looked up to the landing and back down to the living room. They were closer to the top of the stairs than they were to the bottom. Hobbling to the next step up, he said, "You get the first-aid kit. I'll start looking through Darcy's old room."

"At least let me help you," she said.

He unwrapped his arm from Julia's. "You go. I'll get myself upstairs."

"Are you sure?" she asked.

Luis took another step. Man, did that hurt. "I'm positive."

"If you're sure."

He took another step. "Just be careful on the way down."

"And you," she said. "Be careful on the way up."

He tried not to smile.

Julia walked down the stairs, missing the rotten one completely, and disappeared out the front door.

Struggling the rest of the way, he made it to the second floor. There were four doors. The first on the right led to the master suite. The second on the left was for the bathroom. The one next door had belonged to Darcy as a child. According to the notes in the case file, the final room had been a combination junk room and office.

Outside of Darcy's bedroom, Luis stood without movement, or even drawing a breath. He knew there was something different about this house—something sinister about the room. The hairs on the nape of his neck stood on end. Gripping the door-knob, he turned the handle.

Nothing.

He tried again.

The door remained closed.

It wasn't that moisture had left the door swollen shut. The room's lock was actually engaged.

It made no sense. The house had been thoroughly searched several months ago. Nobody in law enforcement would have locked a door. It was easy for Luis to believe that that house had secrets it wasn't willing to share.

After taking a step back, Luis launched himself forward. A bolt of pain shot through his ankle as the wooden frame cracked and the door opened. Stepping inside, he knew instantly that this was the room where all the madness had begun.

Julia stood at the front door. Desperate to rid her lungs of the dankness that permeated the house, she drew in a deep lungful of clean forest air. With the sun overhead, the air was growing warm. Despite the heat, she shivered. Giving a backward glance, she walked across the crumbling porch and made her way to the truck to grab her first-aid kit that was stored behind the single bench seat.

After fidgeting with the release, Julia tipped the seat forward and spied a tackle box with a red cross emblazoned on the lid.

Reaching for the handle, she tried to pull the box free. The latch caught on the back of the seat and the lid sprang open. Gauze, bandages, antibiotic ointment and tape spilled onto the floor. Julia cursed and leaned farther into the truck. Her fingertips brushed an ACE bandage.

She froze and held her breath.

What was that noise?

Was it the crunch of footsteps on gravel?

The skin on the back of her neck tickled. She felt as if she was being watched. Julia slowly backed out and stood. Her gut burned. She could almost feel her lost fingers—phantom limb, the doctors had called the sensation. She reached for her holster and unlatched the snap. Using her left hand, she withdrew the firearm.

Holding her breath, she spun around, arm extended and finger on the trigger.

There was nobody, just the creepy old house, rising like a tombstone out of the overgrown lawn.

Julia laughed, the sound little more than a cackle. "Sheesh, I'm as jumpy as Luis's cat," she chided herself.

After slipping the gun back into the holster, she relatched the snap. She bent back toward the truck, then stopped.

There it was again. A whisper of a sound, so faint it could almost be a breath in her ear. Julia looked up quickly. A movement. She stared through the rear windshield. A face peered back. Standing at the end of the truck's bed, the person was dressed in black. A black hood was pulled up over stringy blond hair, the face was kept in shadow.

It was the same person who'd been in her house.

Her heart hammered, and bile rose in the back of Julia's throat. Cold sweat covered her brow and snaked into her eyes. She blinked as the cold hand of panic gripped her throat and squeezed. Still, she rallied enough to act and not cower.

She backed out of the truck, drawing her sidearm in one movement.

"Police," she said, following protocol. "I'm placing you under arrest for trespassing at my own damn house. And I'm taking you in for questioning in the death of Tom Dolan."

The person took off at a sprint, running for the trees that lined the drive.

"Stop," Julia yelled. In an instant, she assessed that the person was a danger to themselves and others. "Stop," she said again, "or I'll shoot."

The person only ran faster.

She pulled the trigger. Her shoulder jolted with the recoil. The shot went wide, the trunk of a tree exploding with the impact.

With a curse, she gave chase. Her feet slapped the ground as she pushed harder. The figure in front put more distance between them. The trees grew closer to one another, blocking out the light. The temperature dropped. Roots snaked up from the ground. One caught Julia's foot and she stumbled forward. The gun slipped from her grip. It fired as it hit the ground.

The stench of cordite filled Julia's nostrils and her ears began to ring.

Ahead, the person dodged behind a tree and disappeared from Julia's view.

Scrambling to her feet, she awkwardly gathered her gun and set off at a sprint, but stopped at the tree and looked around wildly. Whoever it was, they were gone.

Luis hobbled forward, stepping into Darcy's childhood bedroom. Yellowed curtains hung over grimy windows. A twin bed, complete with a canopy that at one time might have been pink, but was now the color of weak urine, was pressed up against one wall. A small white dresser sat in a corner. A matching vanity with a stool stood at its side against another wall. A shelf of dolls ringed the room. They were covered in dust so thick, it looked like snow.

Obviously, he was standing in a girl's room. Yet, it was well suited for a small child, not a teenager. He knew that Darcy had lived in this house until she was a senior in high school and this space wasn't suitable for a young woman. Then again, there was very little about her upbringing that had been appropriate.

He stepped farther into the room. His ankle ached, throbbing with each beat of his heart.

A small, white metal stool with a velvet cushion was nestled under the vanity. He pulled it out. The cushion slipped. Part of a lid, he supposed. After prying up the top, Luis dumped the contents onto the floor. He picked up an old high school yearbook and flipped through the pages. There were no well wishes written on the sheets reserved for signatures. In the sophomore class, he found an unsmiling picture of

Darcy Owens. Staring at the photo, he wondered if there was a clue in her blank stare. Was she already dead inside, preparing to embark on a life of killing?

Tucked into the back cover was a graduation tassel from thirteen years ago, the same year that the yearbook had been produced. Had it belonged to Robert Carpenter?

He looked through the rest of the cache that had been stored in the stool. Bits of paper. Old candy wrappers. A few pens.

A headless Ken doll and his counterpart, Barbie, with no legs or arms.

Repressing a shiver, Luis lowered himself onto the stool.

As he sat, he saw it in his mind's eye. He'd seen an irregularity just seconds before. What had it been? A slip of paper. Was it a tag on the bottom cushion? He stood. Pain wrapped around his ankle and squeezed. With a curse, he shoved aside the ache and lifted the cushion once again.

Bingo. There was a slip of paper—yellowed and brittle with age—attached to the wooden underside of the cushion. He tugged.

Two things happened at once.

First, the paper disintegrated with his touch.

Second, another inch became exposed. The paper was white, with faint blue lines—the kind found in almost any notebook—and definitely not a tag left by the manufacturer. Moreover, if Darcy had taken great pains to hide this note—and he assumed it was a note—then he also assumed it was important to her state of mind all those years ago.

But he dared not pull anymore, since he could destroy the paper and whatever it might say.

On closer examination, Luis found that the wooden seat bottom was held in place with a series of small staples. He pushed through the thick coating of dust and debris on the top of the vanity and found a set of tweezers, the ends brown with rust.

He worked the flat head of the tweezers under a staple. It popped free. After removing four more staples, Luis peeled back the thin piece of wood. It broke with a crack. A folded sheet of paper clung to the bottom of the cushion. It had been there so long that fibers from both the cloth and the paper had fused, becoming a new creation.

Using the tweezers again, Luis pulled the paper loose and set it on the vanity. It hadn't been a note, but rather the entry from a journal that was dated in November, eleven years ago.

He read the large, looped handwriting and went cold.

> We've decided to do it. The Watcher knows how to make it all look accidental. My dad will look like he died of exposure and then a few weeks—months?—later, my mom will hang herself from grief. I can't believe that this will work, but I hope. I want the nightmare to end.

Luis looked over his shoulder and into the hallway. "Julia," he shouted. "You have to come and see this."

Nothing.

"Julia?"

Luis consulted his phone for the time. How long had she been gone? True, he hadn't noted the time she'd left, yet to him, it seemed like she'd been gone longer than a quick trip to the truck. Which meant what?

"Julia?" he called out again.

Hobbling from the bedroom, Luis carried the note by the nose of the tweezers and crossed the hallway. He entered what had been the master bedroom, which faced the front of the house. He moved to the window and looked down. The pickup truck sat in the drive, with the passenger door open. A first-aid kit was lying on the ground.

But what had happened to Julia? And where had she gone?

Julia's heart hammered hard against her chest. Despite the fact that she knew it to be an impossibility, she feared that her ribs might crack. Her breath came in shallow gasps and her middle ached with each inhalation.

"Where are you?" she whispered. "Show yourself, you coward."

A rustling came from behind. She spun and aimed the revolver. A bird erupted from the scrub and soared to the upper branches of a scraggly pine. Julia tried to laugh. The noise came out as a strangled cry.

She let her shoulder relax and her arm hung at her

side. Julia took a step forward and stopped. Tall trees surrounded her on all sides. The undergrowth was thick, obscuring the forest floor. Her slowing pulse resonated in her skull, and the call of birds filled the air. She searched for something that looked familiar. It was all the same. Trees. Brush. Peeks of blue sky.

"Get a grip, McCloud," she said out loud. Somehow, the sound of her own voice slowed her pulse and cleared her thinking.

Julia knew one thing: she had to save herself. After all, she'd gone through Ranger School. She was now sheriff of Pleasant Pines. She could do this.

With another inhale, she focused and found a set of vines that had been pulled aside at the base of a tree. A scuff mark on the dirt was visible from where she stood. Julia moved to the spot. From there, she looked for another clue to follow. A low branch, broken. She walked toward it. Saw that the broken branch was still damp with sap and knew that the break was recent.

Her heart rate lowered and she scanned the woods once more. There was a felled tree, covered in lichen, that had been kicked loose by a boot heel.

Like a modern-day Gretel from the fairy tale, she picked her way through the woods, moving from one mark to the next. All the while, she thought of what had lured her into the woods. A person. No, not any person. It was whoever'd been following her since Tom Dolan turned up dead in the park.

Julia was the one who found the body.

Was the discovery of the body completely random? Or had Tom Dolan been left there for Julia to find?

And if so, why?

She had to admit she didn't have a single idea. And the implications were too terrifying to consider.

Chapter 11

"Damn it. Damn it. Damn it." Luis cursed with each painful step as he hustled from the house and down the stairs, making sure to avoid the step that had broken.

Bursting through the front door, he placed his hands on either side of his mouth. "Julia?" he called out. "Where are you? *Julia!*"

Standing still, he held his breath and listened.

There was no answer.

He made his way to the truck. The first-aid kit he'd seen from the second-story window was still lying on the ground. The latch was open, but the box was empty. He peered inside the truck. The contents of the first-aid kit were scattered behind the back seat.

Luis immediately catalogued all of the things that might've happened to Julia. Then again, this was a woman who'd served in a combat zone and graduated from Ranger School.

If anyone could handle themselves, it was Julia.

Except, she'd been off since her attack at home. Maybe even before then. Perhaps embroiling herself in the newest murder investigation hadn't been the best idea.

The murder investigation.

Looking at his hand, Luis realized that he still held the diary entry by a set of tweezers. After taking a moment to retrieve a plastic evidence bag from the glove box, Luis slipped both items inside. He tucked the bag into the first-aid kit and set it on the driver's seat.

Stepping away from the truck, he yelled again. "Julia? Can you hear me?"

Nothing.

"Julia?"

His pulse raced as he stepped off the gravel drive and onto the lawn. There, a tree trunk was broken and splintered. He walked to the tree and touched the scarring. Was that a bullet hole?

Who had been shooting? And what had been the intended target?

The woods lightened, and Julia noted that the trees were farther apart. She paused, straining her vision, as she looked for a clearing that might lead to the road…or, better yet, the house.

A beam of light cut through the gloom. A figure moved out of the shadows, skirting the light before disappearing behind another tree.

Sucking in a breath, she dropped to her knee. Certainly, her drab clothes blended with the trees and foliage, yet it was hardly enough to keep her hidden. Lifting the gun, she looked down the sight and tracked the person as they walked away from where she was kneeling. Sweat collected at her hairline and dripped into her eyes. She blinked. It made no difference.

In the army, she'd been trained to take the shot, but only if absolutely certain. The person walked slowly, looking left and right. From where she hid, behind the bushes, the figure had no distinct features. So really, it could be anyone. Yet, who else would it be other than the person Julia had seen at the truck?

Hooking a finger around the trigger, Julia pulled in twice. Smoke rose from the barrel. As if pushed from behind, the figure fell forward.

Holding her gun down and at her side, Julia sprinted to the downed figure. From three yards away, she stopped and felt vomit rise in the back of her throat. The person was no longer indistinct and there wasn't a bit of golden-blond hair.

Holstering her gun, Julia dove through the dirt toward the prone figure.

"Luis," she breathed as she rolled him to his back. His face was covered with grime and blood. "Luis, can you hear me? Where'd you get hit?"

What if she'd hit him in the head? Good Lord,

Julia couldn't live with herself if she'd mistakenly murdered Luis. A pink scrape ran down the ridge of his nose and filled with pinpricks of blood. She ran her hands through his thick, dark hair. She couldn't find a wound.

Groaning, Luis's eyelids fluttered open. "What the hell happened?" he asked, his voice a croak.

"I shot you," said Julia. *Damn it. Get a grip.* She wiped her eyes with her shoulder. "Where'd you get hit?"

"You didn't shoot me," he said. Trying to sit up, he lifted his shoulders from the ground.

Julia firmly pressed him back. "You're in shock," she said. She'd seen it happen more than once in Afghanistan. Soldiers who'd been riddled with bullets stayed on their feet and continued in combat until they could fight no more.

"I'm not in shock." Lifting a hand to his cheek, he picked out a sliver of wood. "I think you hit the tree. I dove for cover when I heard the shots. I must've hit my head and knocked myself out for a few seconds." A purple bruise was starting to form on his forehead, evidence that his scenario was most likely true.

Julia looked up. A rivet had been carved into the side of the tree. Her shot had been close, but not close enough. The other bullet had struck a tree five yards away. Relief washed over Julia in a great wave. "Thank goodness I can't hit the broad side of a barn anymore."

Luis sat up. He looked at his elbow. The fabric of his shirt was ripped, and the skin beneath looked raw.

"I'm so sorry," she said. "It's all my fault."

"I'd rather have a few scrapes on me than a few holes in me." He rose to his feet and dusted off the knees of his pants. "But Julia, why'd you shoot at me in the first place?"

"I thought you were someone else," she said.

"Who else is going to be in the middle of the woods? And why would you want to shoot them in the back?"

"Because," said Julia. "I saw the same person—the hooded intruder—again. The person who was in my house this morning is here now."

Luis narrowed his eyes and scanned the woods. "Tell me exactly what you saw."

They walked a short distance, the silence interrupted only by the far-off calls of birds and their own footfalls in the undergrowth. Julia struggled to explain what had happened.

"I heard something. A step on the gravel drive, maybe. I turned to look..."

"And then," Luis coaxed when Julia's story ebbed into silence.

"And then I looked through the rear windshield, and she was standing at the back of the liftgate."

"And then?" he asked again.

As Julia relayed what had happened, they stepped onto the gravel drive. In the distance, she saw the house's roofline. It meant that they'd exited the woods closer to the road than the Owens homestead. How had she gotten so lost? How had she let her skills become so sloppy?

Then again, Julia knew. Since she'd been attacked—not just this morning, but months ago in the bunker—she'd been afraid. And fear wasn't an emotion she was used to. Sweat collected at the nape of her neck and slithered down her back. "In the woods, something occurred to me."

"Which is?"

"What if placing Tom Dolan in the gazebo wasn't random?" She paused and waited for Luis to say something…anything. He didn't and she continued. "You said it yourself this morning—the person who broke into my house likely timed their break-in to coincide with my run. What if the body was left someplace that I'd find it?"

"Then it sounds like there's a lot more for you to worry about—whoever is following you has killed once." Luis paused. "What if you're their next victim?"

If Luis was right, and he was afraid that he was, then Julia's life was at risk. For a moment, he imagined a world without Julia. The thought hit him with the force of a train that had jumped the tracks. They approached the truck and he tried to think of something to say. There were no words.

And then, his eye was drawn to the first-aid kit that sat on the driver's seat, and more importantly, to the evidence envelope inside. "I found something," he said. Stretching across the seats, Luis opened the kit and retrieved the bag.

"What is it?" Julia asked.

"Proof that Darcy had an accomplice, at least for the killings of her parents."

Taking the envelope, Julia read the diary entry through the translucent plastic. "Who is the Watcher? Bethany Edwards?"

"Yeah, but she has an alibi for Tom Dolan's death."

"Could be another friend."

"Didn't Chloe Ryder work at Darcy's high school? She was a social work intern or something."

With a nod, Julia said, "I think you're right."

"There was a yearbook upstairs," said Luis. "We can take it back to Pleasant Pines and show it to Chloe."

"Don't you think we should search the rest of the house?"

"I think we've done enough. If we need to, we can come back."

She nodded. "I'll get the yearbook."

Luis wasn't about to let Julia out of his sight, not even for a few minutes, especially since she was being stalked by a killer. "I'll go with you," he said.

Thankfully, she didn't argue. Within a few minutes, they'd returned to Darcy's room, retrieved the yearbook and resecured the home. They took a few minutes more to clean and bandage the cut to Luis's leg. The rest of the injuries he left to heal on their own.

"Didn't Robert Carpenter say something about the homecoming dance and a prank that Bethany played?" said Julia, flipping through the pages of the yearbook.

"Yeah, that Bethany cut off all of Darcy's hair. And then today, Bethany denied it all. We decided that either Robert or Bethany is lying."

"Here's an easy way to find out which one," said Julia. She opened the yearbook to the section that covered the homecoming festivities. Pep rally. Football game. Parade. "Ah, the dance."

Luis looked over her shoulder as they scoured the pictures. Second page, bottom left corner. There was a picture of two kids, holding hands and awkwardly dancing. He read the caption. "'Senior Robert Carpenter with his date, Darcy Owens.'"

"Looks like Darcy attended the dance after all," said Julia.

"It also looks like Robert lied to us," he replied. "I think we need to pay him a visit."

"This morning, Robert Carpenter told us that he grew up near Darcy," said Julia as she slid behind the steering wheel of the truck. "I wonder if his parents still own the house? It'll be an easy drive and who knows what they might say."

Luis nodded, but his mind was elsewhere. If Tom Dolan's killer was really stalking Julia, then for Luis, learning the killer's identity had gone from a professional priority to a personal one.

Finding Robert Carpenter's home hadn't been difficult. Exactly as he told Julia and Luis earlier in the day, he did live down the road from Darcy.

The house sat atop a rise. At the bottom of a gravel

drive that led to the home there was a mailbox with the name Robert Carpenter.

"You think he bought his parents' house?" Luis asked as Julia let her truck idle on the empty road. "Or is he a Junior?"

"I think this might be his house," said Julia. "He gave me his card." She fished it from her pocket and held it out for Luis to see. "It says Robert E. Carpenter. I think a guy like that would include his full name."

"Well, there's only one way to find out," he said as Julia parked on the road's shoulder.

There were no cars parked near the front door. A metal swing set and aboveground pool—covered with a tarp for the coming winter—filled a side yard. Several newspapers, rolled and tucked into plastic sleeves, sat on the stoop.

Walking up the drive with Luis at her side, Julia took time to study the property. It was a split-entry home, covered with vinyl siding and brick. Curtains were open at almost every window. Not a light could be seen, and she didn't notice any movement.

From where she stood, Julia would swear that nobody was home.

Yet, looks could be deceiving.

She knocked on the door. "Mr. Carpenter. It's Julia McCloud. I'd like to have a word with you."

Nothing.

She knocked again, louder this time. The door's frame rattled.

“Mr. Carpenter. Sheriff McCloud. I have some questions.”

She waited and knocked once more.

She’d been right—nobody was home.

“Tuck a card into the door. Hopefully, when he gets home, he’ll call,” said Luis.

Julia did as he suggested and added her cell-phone number on the back, along with a note that he should call ASAP.

“There might be one more place where we should check before going back to Pleasant Pines.” She removed Robert E. Carpenter’s card and held it out. “He works at an auto-parts store nearby.”

“Then let’s go and check it out,” said Luis.

The trip to Robert Carpenter’s work proved as fruitless as stopping by his house. He wasn’t scheduled to work until the following day and his employees couldn’t reach him on his cell phone.

Luis offered to drive back to Pleasant Pines and Julia let him. She needed a little time to think about what had happened over the last day and half. More than the stalker invading her home, she wondered why Robert Carpenter would come to her office and tell a story that could easily be proven to be a lie.

It made no sense…unless, he had something to hide.

And she intended to find out what it was.

Luis pulled onto Main Street in Pleasant Pines just as the dashboard clock changed to 5:05 p.m. Sure, they’d been chasing down leads for several hours.

Yet it seemed like they'd been gone for days, or even months. Pulling to a stop in an empty spot behind the county office building, he killed the engine.

Turning his attention to the matter of the investigation, he lifted the evidence bag. "Let's see if Chloe's in her office."

"Agreed," said Julia.

The district attorney's office was located on the ground floor in the county office building. They entered the office without knocking. The space was a mirror image of the sheriff's department, which was one floor up. There was a large outer office with several desks and a single inner office.

From the doorway, Luis spied Chloe sitting behind her desk. "Gotta minute?" he asked as he approached. He'd tucked the evidence bag into the yearbook and was holding both in a loose grip.

"Sure thing," said Chloe as she stood. "What can I help you with?"

Luis moved into the office and Julia followed. She pulled the door shut.

"A closed door?" Chloe asked with a lifted eyebrow. "This seems serious."

"It is," said Martinez. He set the note on Chloe's desk.

Placing her palms on each side of the bag, she read and her eyes widened. "Where did you get this?"

"It was hidden under the cushion of a vanity stool at Darcy Owens's childhood home."

"In her bedroom," Julia added.

"You think this came from what? A diary belonging to Darcy Owens?" Chloe asked as she studied the document.

"You don't?" Julia replied.

Chloe sighed. "It might. Then again, it might not. Did you find the rest of the diary?"

"What does it matter?" Julia asked. "You can tell from the context of the letter that it's from Darcy, and that she had an accomplice in killing her parents."

"If you had the complete diary, somehow attributed to Darcy Owens, and this—a missing and matching page—then we can possibly say that she wrote this. Then, it would have to be tested for the date, and examined by a handwriting expert..."

Luis held up his hands. "I get it, Chloe. You're thinking like a lawyer—"

"I am a lawyer," she interrupted.

He continued, "You want what's admissible in court or to find problems with evidence that might be challenged, but that's not what we need now."

Julia said, "What we need is a name to go with whoever is the Watcher. You worked at Darcy's high school, right? You must remember if there was anyone with whom Darcy was close."

Chloe slowly shook her head. "That was more than a decade ago. I'm not sure that I recall much that would be helpful." She reached for the yearbook and flipped through the pages. "Let me see if anything jogs my memory." With a sigh, she held out the book after a few minutes. "Sorry, I can't be more helpful."

Julia took the offered book and left the office. As she walked up the stairs, she said, "Let's put this and the diary entry into the evidence locker. Then we can regroup and devise a new plan."

The door to the sheriff's office was closed and locked. A handwritten sign hung on the door—Gone for the Night.

He lifted the paper from the door. "You'd never see something like this in Denver. The patrol room was never quiet, much less empty."

"Do you miss all the busyness of your old life?" she asked while entering a combination into the lock.

Luis didn't even consider his answer. "Not at all."

Holding the door open, she said, "After you."

Chuckling, he paused as he passed her. "Thanks."

Their gazes met.

Adrenaline rushed through his system, until it felt as if his blood ran with an electric charge. Swallowing, he looked at the floor and focused on the corner of a cracked tile. "You have a code for the evidence room?" he asked, hooking his thumb toward a small door in the corner.

"Of course." Julia entered a code on the door's lock and turned the handle.

The evidence room was little more than a closet—three walls covered by shelves that were filled with boxes. She pulled the door closed, leaving them safely ensconced with all the evidence…and cut off from the rest of the world. A card with case file numbers, dates and the suspect's name was attached to the end of each box. Half of one wall was reserved for Darcy's files.

Luis removed the most recent box and slid the

diary entry and yearbook inside. He then wrote a note about the material and ended the notation with his initials. In the small space, Julia's breath washed over his shoulder. He turned. She was there, close but not yet touching. Her aroma—musk, wildflowers and an underlying note that was wholly female—surrounded him. Luis was slightly drunk on her scent.

The room was suddenly too small. The air was too hot, and his skin was too tight. In a flash, he saw them tangled in an embrace. Felt her naked thighs wrapped around his waist.

What was he thinking? Julia was…well, Julia.

His friend. His confidante. His companion.

He couldn't be having fantasies about her while they were locked in a tiny closet. And yet, his eyes were drawn to her lips. He inched closer.

What the hell? He had to get away.

Reaching for the handle, Luis pushed open the door. He stepped into the squad room and moved to the opposite wall. Sitting on the desk's edge, he drew in a lungful of air.

"You okay?" Julia asked while closing the door and engaging the lock. "You look like you got spooked in there."

He shook his head. "I'm okay."

"You sure? Is your ankle bothering you?"

"It's fine."

"What is it, then?"

What was he supposed to say? That he wondered what it would feel like to hold Julia in his arms? Or that he was dying to find out how her kisses might taste?

"Maybe I'm just hungry. We never stopped for lunch."

"You go home. Get something to eat. We've done good work for the day and can pick up tomorrow where we've left off."

"Come with me," he said, rising to his feet. "You haven't eaten, either."

"I've got work to do. Calls to make."

"You need to eat sometime, otherwise you won't be effective. You know that," said Luis. And, sure, what he said was true. Julia needed to eat to stay healthy. But there were other reasons why he encouraged her to join him.

Simply put, he liked spending time in her company.

And, yeah, okay, she was really easy to look at.

Early on, Luis had drawn a line that kept them both safely in the friend zone.

But what happened when the line between friends and lovers was becoming harder to maintain?

Chapter 12

Julia knew that Luis was right. If she wanted to be effective, she needed to eat. Without fuel, even the fastest car in the world would quit running. Despite piles of work still waiting for her attention, she gave in. Together, Julia and Luis walked down the street to the diner, Sally's on Main.

Every seat at the long counter was occupied. All of the tables were full, as well. The scent of something salty and fried hung in the air, and Julia's stomach grumbled painfully.

Sally, the owner and namesake of the diner, approached. "Evening, folks."

"How's Sarge?" Julia asked.

"He and Gunner are settled. It'll be nice to have him around the house for a few days." Then she asked, "Is it just you two or will others be meeting you?"

"Just the two of us," said Luis.

A table in the back cleared out. "Give me a second to get that cleaned off for you."

"Thanks, Sal," he said. Within a minute, both Julia and Luis were seated and had been served drinks—water for Luis and a steaming cup of coffee for Julia.

"Sally and Sarge," said Julia, smiling. "I like them as a couple."

"Sure, they're cute, but that coffee will keep you up all night, you know," said Luis, tapping a finger on the side of Julia's cup.

Lifting the mug to her lips, she took a sip. "That's what I'm hoping. I've got hours' more work to do before I can call it quits." Plus, she was afraid of what nightmares might lurk.

Luis's gaze traveled around the restaurant. "When I was a cop, I did my best work in a little convenience store in my neighborhood back in Denver. It was a shop, not a restaurant, but it reminds me a lot of Sally's." He sipped his water and continued. "A bunch of guys hung out at the store and I stopped every morning for a newspaper."

"Why didn't you get one delivered?" Julia took another swallow of coffee. Caffeine buzzed through her veins. "It'd save you time in the morning."

"Not all news is in the papers. Look around. Thomas Irwin, from the bank, is here. He works with everyone in town. Sally knows everyone and their personal business, I bet. Hell, the editor of the paper is even at the counter. You should work the room a little."

"I'm the sheriff, not some damn politician," said Julia, though she suspected that Luis was right. She took another sip of coffee. "And I'm definitely not talking to the newspaper's editor."

"Why not?"

"You saw that hit job he did on you with that story. How am I supposed to trust the guy?"

"Did he release some embarrassing facts about me?" he asked, then answered his own question. "Sure, he did. Was he wrong? Sadly, no." While picking a lemon seed from his water, Luis continued. "I ruined my own life. It's not the newspaper's fault. Besides, in a small way, I'm glad it came out."

"Really? Because I'm mad that he embarrassed you like that. And ambushed me in the early morning, too."

Luis looked up and pinned Julia with his stare. His eyes were a deep and warm brown. Her fingers itched with the need to touch him. Her whole body tingled with the need to have him touch her in return. "To be honest, I'm moved that you care so much."

Was there something in his words? Something more than camaraderie? Did she dare to broach the subject of…feelings? "Of course, I care."

"Honestly, I'm glad you're here. You're a good friend, Julia."

Friends. Great.

She shook her head as if to clear it, then nodded

and took a sip of coffee. "This morning, you said you don't speak to your family anymore. Do you miss your sister?"

"Of course."

"Why don't you call her and apologize? You've changed. Besides, I bet she misses you, too."

"I suppose that's it—what if I haven't changed? Or I haven't changed enough?"

Julia's chest ached with Luis's pain.

"You're handling this all remarkably well. Me, I still can't get over what Peter did."

"That's one of the first steps to moving forward—owning your past." Luis added, "Besides, Peter Knowles is good at his job. He found out about me. I wonder what such a good reporter might be able to dig up about Darcy's childhood?"

Thankfully, she was saved from adding anything else to the conversation by the arrival of a server. "What can I get for you this evening? The special is chicken-fried steak with potatoes and gravy. Green beans come as the side. I had some before my shift. It's really good. You should try it, Sheriff."

"Sold," said Julia.

"Make that two." After the server left, Luis leaned back. "See?"

"'See' what?" Although Julia suspected that she knew what Luis was about to say.

"Even the waitress at Sally's knows who you are. You'll have to get used to all the hand shaking. Making friends and influencing people—that's your job now."

Julia grunted.

"I'm not comfortable in the spotlight. I like to make things happen and see results. Other people can take the credit. I just want to do my job and keep my life private."

"Being sheriff of a town that is recovering from a spate of serial killings—and with a new murder, no less—is hardly the place to avoid being a public figure."

"That's what I'm worried about."

The door to the restaurant opened. Sean Reynolds entered, accompanied by three other men. Julia recognized them all as friends of Tom Dolan. She watched them take seats at a booth near the door. "Give me a sec." She rose and moved through the restaurant, not entirely sure what she planned to say to the group of men. But she knew that she had to say something.

She approached the table. "Hey, Sean. Hey, fellas. How're you holding up?"

"Lousy," said Sean. He scooted over on the bench, making room for Julia. "Any news on the investigation?"

She slid into the seat. "I really don't have much to report. Right now, we're waiting for results from the toxicology reports. Sometimes, they can take weeks. Months, even. I've asked that the tests be expedited and am hoping we have answers tomorrow or Wednesday. Obviously, we're most interested in finding the blond woman. I spent time following up on leads today, but nothing definitive." She paused. "How much longer are you staying in town?"

"I'm saving my in-laws the heartache of bringing Tom's body home. I'll be here until the body's released for transport. The guys have all agreed to stay with me…and him."

"That's a wonderful gesture." Julia's heart went out to him. She squeezed his arm, just a slight pressure, to show that she saw and understood his pain and anguish. "I'll get back to you as soon as I know something. If you guys think of anything at all that might help, give me a call."

"Will do," said Sean.

Julia rose to her feet and walked toward the table. Peter Knowles stepped into her path. He had the nerve to smile. "I thought I saw you come in."

"I still have no comment, and I doubt I ever will. That story was crap."

"Are you saying it isn't true? I'd love to chat with you and Mr. Martinez. How's the investigation going? Do you have a minute?"

Without a word, Julia brushed past the newspaperman. On her way to the table, Thomas Irwin—manager of the local bank—waved her over and introduced Julia to his wife and kids. He told her about the Halloween party the bank would be hosting—letting kids trick-or-treat at the teller's windows—and invited Julia to stop by. "There'll be cider and donuts," Thomas promised.

"I'll put it on my calendar," she said, knowing that Luis would insist she attend. At the same time, she wondered if he'd come with her.

The town dentist was also having a late dinner, and he said hello.

Several ranchers, all sitting in a row at the counter, had complaints about a mountain lion that was killing their livestock. The elementary-school principal came to Julia's table and invited her to speak at career day the second week in November. When she finally made it back to the table, she barely had time to eat.

After they paid for the meal, Luis and Julia stepped onto the sidewalk. Streetlights glowed and a mist hung in the air, accentuating the strong tang of pine from the nearby woods. Walking to the county office building, Luis asked, "That wasn't so bad, was it?"

Julia gave him a sidelong glance. "Bad? I shook more hands this evening than I have my entire life." He laughed and Julia's insides tightened—and not in a bad way. "Well, I better get back to work." She gestured toward the steps that led to the front door.

"You need any more help?"

Julia shook her head. "I'm going to follow up with Bethany Edwards's boyfriend and the names that Candace Johnson gave me." There was something else she wanted to do, but Julia kept those plans to herself.

"You sure?"

"I'm sure."

"Also, the offer from before still stands. You can crash at my place."

"Thanks, but really, I'm good. I've lived with the

fear of Darcy Owens for too long. I'm not going to let someone else make me afraid." Julia almost believed her own bravado. Yet, flashbacks to the person hiding in her bathroom and the breathless chase through the woods came to mind. She pushed them all away. "I'm good, really."

"All right, then. G'night."

"G'night," said Julia. She climbed the steps to the front door of the county office building. She paused. There was something she wanted to tell Luis, but she couldn't quite find the right words. Finally, she glanced over her shoulder, but Luis was already gone.

Peter sat at the counter and scraped his fork across the plate. He'd been eating at Sally's since he was a kid and, hand to God, he never got tired of the food. But there was more than just burgers and cakes on the menu. Sally's was the best place to pick up on town gossip, which often led to bona fide news stories.

And as far as Peter could tell, one of the biggest stories was sitting in a booth near the door. Peter left money on the counter for both his meal and a tip, then walked toward the table. Four men looked up as he approached.

Peter already had a business card in his hand. "I'm sorry to bother you," he said, handing over his card to the guy named Sean. "But from the sheriff, I understand that you're the brother-in-law of the man discovered at the park on Sunday." It wasn't a lie at all. Peter had overheard what Julia said, thus making her his source. Turning his attention to the table and the four men, he added, “I’m sorry for your loss.”

“Thanks,” said Sean. “Tom was a good guy.”

“Mind if I ask you all a few questions? I’m writing a story about Tom—” thank goodness he now had a name “—and what happened. I can talk to the sheriff, but always feel that speaking to folks firsthand is best.”

Sean glanced around the table. Everyone gave a quick nod. “Sure.”

Peter took an empty chair from a nearby table and placed it at the end of the booth. He removed a pad of paper and pen from his blazer pocket and sat. “So,” he began, “what can you tell me about Tom?”

For the next thirty minutes, Peter took notes. Because as luck would have it, all four men had a lot to say.

Julia placed the phone back onto the receiver. She’d spent the last hour making calls and verifying alibis. So far, she’d spoken to Bethany Edwards’s new boyfriend, who’d corroborated her story of a quiet night at home. Likewise, Candace Johnson’s friends also claimed to have ridden in Bethany’s loaned car.

It wasn’t a surprise that Bethany’s alibi checked out. Still, it gave her nothing to follow up. Julia stretched and checked the time—8:30 p.m.

Nobody would think her weak if she left work now, would they?

Then again, Tom Dolan deserved justice.

More than that, Julia wanted to know who in the hell was using Darcy's MO to kill again.

Both were noble causes and worthy of her time, but how much more would she accomplish tonight?

Not much, she knew, and that was the problem.

Then again, there was something she could get done. Turning in her chair, Julia powered up her computer and opened the law-enforcement database. True, she wasn't supposed to access this information for personal reasons, but Luis was a professional colleague as well as a friend.

That made finding his sister's phone number part of the job, right?

With the information on the screen, Julia reached for her phone and dialed the number.

A woman answered. "Hello?"

"Hi, Francesca. This is Julia McCloud. I'm the sheriff in Pleasant Pines, Wyoming. I'm calling because of your brother, Luis."

She exhaled loudly. "Whatever he did, I can't help him…or you. I haven't spoken to Luis in years."

"Your brother isn't in any kind of trouble. In fact, I've been working with him for the better part of a year and, well, I think he's changed."

Francesca snorted. "Doubt it."

Julia could feel the other woman's resistance, even over the phone line, but pressed ahead. "I met Luis in Denver, right after he started going to Gamblers Anonymous. Since then, he's brought a drug kingpin to justice. He's tracked down a killer. He actually saved my life, too."

Pausing, Julia waited for Francesca to fill the void. The other woman said nothing.

She could easily quit while behind. It was just that Julia hated losing, and really, she'd lost so much up until now. "This morning I found out that he struggles with an addiction to gambling. And that his problems destroyed his relationship with you, and others, too. He doesn't know I'm calling. But every day, your brother risks his life for someone else. I think he's trying to make up for all his mistakes."

Julia's words were met with more silence. Had Luis's sister hung up the phone? "Hello? Are you there?"

"Yeah." *Sigh.* "Listen, I appreciate you calling me. I'm glad he's doing good. I'm glad he has a good friend like you, too. But I'm not ready to forgive him—not yet."

"I understand," said Julia. Well, it was worth a try. "Let me give you my cell number if you ever want to talk." Julia could hear Francesca writing as she spoke.

"Thanks," said the other woman. "And tell my brother…" She drew in a deep breath. "Just tell him to be careful, okay?"

"Will do." Julia placed the phone back on the cradle.

True, it wasn't the rebuilt bridge that she hoped to offer Luis. But maybe Julia had helped a little.

Finished for the night, Julia turned off her computer and stood.

A *thump*, like a book hitting the floor, came from the outer office.

Julia froze and her blood ran cold.

"Who's out there?" she called. If the killer had come to her office, Julia was prepared to take a stand. Drawing the gun from its holster, she called out, "Show yourself."

"You still here, Julia?" It was Travis Cooper. She shoved the gun back as her office door opened. "I just finished a patrol. Drove out to Sergeant Taylor's place. No sign of Christopher Booth, or anyone else, for that matter."

"Thanks for checking," she said, though her heart still raced. "Hey, did you hear something?"

"That was me," he said sheepishly. "I tried to set my bag on the desk but missed entirely. Damn dark, I can't see a thing."

Julia tried to smile. "I was just heading out. How's Cassidy?"

"She's worried about the upcoming trial. Doesn't want to face all those creeps who kidnapped her daughter, and still—she has no choice."

Julia knew which trial Travis was talking about. While the leader of the Transgressors had escaped, most of the other men had been taken into custody. Cassidy, having rescued the women with Travis, had been asked to testify. "Maybe Cassidy will get lucky. Maybe all the Transgressors will take a plea deal and there won't be a trial."

"We can only hope, right?"

"Right," said Julia. "You need anything before I leave?"

"Just gonna wait here and see if any calls come in. If not, I'll run another patrol in a few hours. I should be good until morning."

"See you then," said Julia.

After collecting her jacket, keys and duffel bag, Julia left the office. Standing on the threshold, Julia's heart slammed into her ribs. The hallway was long and dark. She wiped a shaking hand over her damp brow.

She glanced into the office. Sitting at a desk with his feet up, Travis scrolled through his phone. Sure, she could go back and talk to the deputy. Then again, she had to leave sometime. It's just that Julia didn't want to go home—not tonight, anyway.

If not home, where could she stay?

Then again, she knew the perfect place.

Night had come to Pleasant Pines, turning the sky a dusty purple, bathing the surrounding mountains in black. All of the downtown businesses were closed. Lampposts cast golden circles of light on the street below Luis's apartment.

Sitting on the sofa with a tepid beer in hand, Luis stared at the TV. A baseball game was on the screen, but he paid no attention to the action. Instead, he examined each fact of the investigation, visualizing it as a piece to a puzzle. He tried to make them all fit and form a continuous narrative. Yet each story had significant gaps.

He lifted his phone from the table and called his coworker, Wyatt Thornton.

"You've worked the Darcy Owens case from the beginning, right?"

"Her serial murders first appeared on the radar in Las Vegas. That was my case with the behavioral-sciences unit. So, yeah, I've been on the case since law enforcement was involved."

Adrenaline coursed through Luis's system, like electricity being pumped into his veins. "In all of those cases, did you ever find the victim's ID, or the half of a two-dollar bill, anywhere other than on the body?"

"To be honest," said Wyatt, "I don't think so."

Luis paused. "We found the newest victim's ID in his hotel room. Does that strike you as strange?"

"A little," said Wyatt. "Think about this, if the victim was inebriated, he could've dropped his wallet almost anywhere."

"True. Can you do me a favor? Can you review all the old cases? See if any other victims were found without an ID."

"I'm still here at RMJ and can do it now," said Wyatt. "I assume that you have a theory."

"I might. Then again, I might not. What I do know is that all serial killers like symmetry. An ID being left in the hotel room seems like a zig that is usually a zag."

"I'll see what I can find," said Wyatt.

"Thanks," said Luis. The phone beeped with an

incoming call. "I gotta go." He hung up with Wyatt and glanced at the caller ID. "Julia?"

"Come to your window," she said.

"My what?" He rose from the sofa. His ankle throbbed and he cursed softly with each step. Jinxy, who'd been sitting on an adjacent chair, ran away. Luis stood at the window and pulled back the curtains. Julia stood on the street, a six-pack of beer in one hand and her phone in the other. "I heard there was a game on tonight and thought you'd like a beer and some company."

"I'd love both," he said, unable to hold back his smile. "I'll come down and let you in."

"Don't bother," she said. "Throw down your keys."

He laughed but opened the window and tossed the keys to Julia. She'd set down the beer and caught the keyring one-handed. "I'll be right up," she said, and then ended the call.

Seconds later, there was a knock on Luis's door. "Come in," he called out. "It's open."

"Hey," said Julia. Aside from her beer, she still had the duffel bag from earlier in the day. She set both on the kitchen table. With a purr, Jinxy sauntered out from her hiding place. "Hi, kitty," said Julia as she bent down to pet the cat. The feline wound her lithe body around Julia's legs.

"I think the cat likes you better than she likes me," said Luis. "She says hello to you. All I get is scratched when her food dish is empty."

Julia ruffled Jinxy's ears.

Gesturing to the sofa, Luis said, "Game's on. Have a seat."

Carrying the cat and beer with her, Julia sat at the end of the sofa. "Who's playing?"

"Colorado. Is there another team?" Dropping into a recliner, he asked, "Everything okay?"

"Today has left me jumpy. The thought of sitting at home alone wasn't appealing." She twisted off the bottle cap and took a swallow of beer. "I thought of where else I'd like to be and, well, it was with you."

Was that an invitation? Had Julia felt the connection Luis felt in the evidence locker?

Or was he just hoping she'd say the things that he wanted to hear?

His phone rang and shimmied across the table, interrupting whatever he couldn't bring himself to say. Luis glanced at the screen, then answered and turned on the speaker function.

"Wyatt," he said. "I'm here with Julia. Do you have some news for us?"

"Actually," said Wyatt, "I do. I looked through all of files on Darcy's victims and searched for someone who wasn't identified immediately because they didn't have a wallet with them."

"Like Tom Dolan? Did you find someone?" Julia's eyes were bright.

"I did and I didn't."

Luis asked, "What's that supposed to mean?"

"All of the confirmed victims had their wallets with them when their bodies were found. Moreover, each of them had the half two-dollar bill inside of the wallet, as well. But there was one person I suspected she killed but have never had any proof. It's her father."

Wyatt continued, "It took a little digging. According to the police report from Frank Owens's death, he didn't have any ID on him when he was brought into the morgue. His wife filed a missing person's report and the police assumed—rightly so—that they had discovered the man's identity. When the wife arrived, she brought her husband's wallet with his driver's license. The contents were cataloged then."

"Let me guess," said Julia. "There was half of a two-dollar bill inside."

"Just a footnote on the report," Wyatt replied.

"So what does that mean for this newest investigation?" Luis asked.

"It means that whoever killed Tom Dolan knew intimately about the murder of her father, and yet they hadn't been connected with her in years." Wyatt paused. "We assumed that already. But this is proof positive."

"That should be good news," said Luis. "But you don't sound happy."

"Recent murders are hard enough to solve, much less one that happened more than a decade ago."

"Actually, we do have a witness to the murder of Frank Owens," said Julia. "It's Darcy." She exhaled slowly, as if trying to control her pulse or work up the energy for an amazing feat. Luis supposed that she was doing both. "We have to talk to her and see what she'll say."

Luis knew that Julia was right—they were going to have to talk to the killer. But it didn't mean he had to like it.

In order to solve Tom Dolan's murder, Julia would have to face Darcy Owens—her worst nightmare. And there was nothing Luis could do to protect her… and that was a nightmare all his own.

Chapter 13

The six-pack was empty, and the game was over.

"I meant what I said on Saturday," said Luis to Julia. "I can give you tips on the grip you use on your gun. That'll help you aim."

The comment seemed out of the blue. But it was undeniable: Julia needed help. She'd been a fool not to take it once, but she wasn't about to be a fool again. And there was no time like the present.

"Thanks," she said, rising from her spot on the sofa. She'd stowed her firearm in the duffel bag and now removed it. She withdrew the magazine before pulling back on the slide and taking out the single chambered round. "I'd love some pointers."

"Pick a target."

Julia aimed at the TV.

"Anything other than my big screen. Jeez, you do know how to injure a man's soul," he teased. "Honestly, find a smaller target."

Julia laughed and picked a lamp.

Luis stood right beside her. "Now aim."

She lined up the sight. Luis touched the spot where the barrel pointed. The shot would've gone wide and punched a hole in the wall. "There are two problems," said Luis. "First, you're used to drawing the gun across your body from the right. For the left..." He put his hands on her arm and the shoulder and elbow. Her flesh warmed and tingled with his touch. "You need to put the gun here."

Julia felt the pull in her back as she lined up the sight for a second time.

"See the difference?"

She nodded. "I do."

"The second thing is in your shoulder. The left is your weaker side, so when you pull the trigger, your shoulder is thrown off by the recoil. You need to keep your shoulder stronger." He pulled her arm back and to the side. Luis stood so close that his chest brushed against her back. His breath washed over her shoulder and she couldn't help but wonder what it would feel like if his lips were on her neck.

Cripes. She shouldn't be thinking about Luis like that—no matter that he had broad shoulders, strong arms, a tight behind...

She stepped forward, her throat raw and her pulse racing. "Both tips are useful. Thanks for the help." She waited a beat. "How'd you know what to suggest?"

"Easy, I taught firearms at the police academy in Denver before joining the detective bureau. Plus, I saw you shoot on Saturday. It wasn't hard to diagnose the problem."

Julia shoved her gun back into the duffel bag. She gave a soft laugh. "I guess that'll teach me to not accept help when offered."

"And speaking of help, now's probably the time for both of us to get some sleep. I'm exhausted." He yawned, as if to prove his point. "You take my room." Luis held up his hand before she had a chance to protest. "I insist."

"Good night, then." She lifted her bag from the table. "Thanks for letting me borrow your room."

Julia wandered down the short hallway to Luis's bedroom. Jinxy followed at a trot and jumped on the bed as soon as she turned on the light. After setting the bag on the floor, she removed her gun. Lifting it, she aimed at one of the bricks on the wall. Now aware, she felt the outward roll of her shoulder. Julia moved her arm farther across her body, until her aim was perfect. She aimed again, repeating the motion until it was natural and fluid.

It felt as if she'd reclaimed a piece of herself…and maybe she had. And it was all thanks to Luis. Moving to the window, she looked down at the street. It was empty, and yet, she didn't feel safe.

Then again, she was with Luis and she knew that he'd protect her with his life.

The thought was reassuring, and she pulled the curtains closed. The room was bathed in a warm glow. Jinxy was lying on the bed, her orange tail twitching. Julia disrobed. Wearing only her panties, her eyes dropped to her middle and the scar that bisected her abdomen. A memento from Darcy Owens. It was a like a line on a map, leading straight to hell. Rummaging through her bag, Julia found a pair of shorts and a T-shirt for sleeping.

Slipping beneath the covers, Julia settled her head on the pillow. She drew a deep breath, the scent of Martinez filling her. Closing her eyes, she began to drift to sleep. And in her dreams, she was held tightly in Luis's protective arms.

Hidden in the shadows of a building, the Watcher stood on the street and stared at the window. A figure moved past before pulling the curtains closed. It was Julia. A moment later, the lights went dark. Obviously, she wasn't going home. But how long would she be staying here?

Turning in a slow circle, the Watcher looked up and down the block—gaze settling on a building directly across the street. In the front window was a sign—Apartment for Rent. Immediately Available. The lettering was faded. The edges of the sign had curled and yellowed with the sun. Probably the sign had been taped to the window for several weeks, if not months.

After taking two steps back, the Watcher realized that the buildings were mirror images of one another. The first two floors housed businesses, with the third floor reserved for a residence.

At the back of the building, there was a separate entrance to the apartment. A padlock held a bolt in place, but the wood around the hinges was old. A pocketknife was used to pick away the rotten wood, until the hinges swung free.

The Watcher tensed, waiting for the wail of an alarm.

The night remained silent.

A back staircase led directly to the apartment and another locked door. The Watcher kicked the handle. The wood cracked. The noise echoed all along the stairwell as the door swung open. The scent of new carpeting and fresh paint hung in the air. A set of tall windows faced the opposite side of the street.

From that vantage point, it was easy to see Luis Martinez, sprawled out on a sofa and staring at a TV. Colors washed over him as his eyes drifted closed.

There was nothing else to see, yet the Watcher stayed at the window. In the reflection Darcy stood in the room and smiled. Every breath drew her in. With each heartbeat, Darcy's soul became stronger. They were merging, the Watcher knew. *You've done good,* she whispered. *Now, you have to show me your love. Now, you have to destroy them all.*

The vacant apartment was the perfect location to see and know everything.

In short, the Watcher was now God.

The day dawned overcast, and a light rain started to fall just as the sun would have crested over the horizon and brightened the Wyoming sky. Luis stirred and pain shot from his hips to his knees. Damn. The sofa wasn't meant for someone his size, or a guy who played football for years. Still, a little discomfort didn't matter, especially if Julia had been able to sleep.

Standing in the kitchen, already dressed in jeans and a T-shirt, she was brewing a cup of coffee.

He must've made enough noise that she knew he was awake. With a smile, she looked over her shoulder. "Morning," she said.

"Morning," he mumbled as she set the coffee in front of him. It was black, just like he drank it. Taking a sip, Luis knew it would be easy to get used to having Julia around. "How are you? How do you feel? Did you sleep?"

"Actually, I slept perfectly." Julia reached her arms above her head and arched her back. At this early hour, she hadn't bothered with a bra. Her breasts pressed into the thin fabric of her shirt. He tried not to look. "No nightmares. You wouldn't believe how long it's been since I had a full night's sleep. It must be the fact that I'm here—with you."

With you. What did she mean by that?

Jinxy jumped onto the sofa. The cat placed her head in Luis's hand, and he rubbed her ears.

"And I'm here with Jinxy," said Julia. She joined Luis on the couch and rubbed the cat's head.

Luis couldn't help but smile.

Julia continued, "I was thinking about the plan for today. I still think that speaking to Darcy Owens is the next step in this case."

He knew it, too. "You should call her attorney. Or better yet, get Chloe Ryder to make the arrangements."

"I'm way ahead of you." Julia slipped her phone from her pocket. "I texted Chloe. She's going to make calls and get back to me." The phone pinged with an incoming text.

"That was fast," said Luis.

"It's a text from Doc Lambert." Julia began reading. "He's got some results from Tom Dolan's tests back already," she informed him. "He wants us to stop by the morgue."

"Get ready," said Luis. "And we'll get started. Today's going to be another long day."

It took less than thirty minutes for both Julia and Luis to shower, get ready and eat breakfast. Since his apartment was in the middle of downtown Pleasant Pines, they walked to the hospital under a gray sky that spit cold rain.

The morgue was located in the basement and they descended a staircase that led to a white-tiled hallway. Halfway down the corridor, a blue plastic sign hung from a set of chains. Morgue.

Luis shouldered open one of the stainless-steel doors and entered the room. The floor and walls were covered in the same white tiles as the hallway. One wall was taken up by a set of sinks and a long steel counter. The opposite wall was filled with metal coolers, used to store bodies. In the middle of the floor was a gurney. A blue cloth was draped over the stretcher and a body was beneath.

Doc Lambert stood at the sink, entering information into a tablet computer.

"Morning, Doc," said Luis as the older man looked up.

He nodded a greeting to both Luis and Julia.

"Thanks to the calls made by the DA, we were able to get the toxicology tests expedited." Doc Lambert set aside the tablet. "Well, it seems as though the deceased had a large amount of alcohol in his system."

"I'm not surprised," said Luis. "I could smell the booze on him."

"Is that it?" asked Julia.

"I'm afraid not. We found trace amounts of the same anti-nausea medication Darcy Owens used on her victims, as well." Doc Lambert concluded, "This death is consistent with all the others of Darcy Owens."

Darcy had poisoned her victims by lulling them into a drunken stupor with large amounts of alcohol. Then, she slipped them an anti-nausea med to keep them from expelling the booze as a body would naturally do. It was devious to make it look like all the deaths were natural overdoses and one way that her murders had gone undetected for years.

The facts were all pointing in the same direction. "But it can't be Darcy," said Luis. "Because she's in jail. But it's someone who knew her…and knew her well."

Julia turned to the doctor. "Can Tom Dolan's body be released?"

"Now it can," he said.

"Good," said Julia. She was already walking toward the door. "I'm going to call Sean Reynolds… and then, we have to do it."

Luis knew what she meant by *it*. They had to go and speak to Darcy Owens, a notorious serial killer.

Like the childhood game of telephone, arrangements had been made. Julia had called Chloe. Chloe had called Darcy's attorney, who then contacted his client.

Would Darcy be willing to talk to the sheriff of Pleasant Pines about a recent killing?

The answer came back the same way it went out. Sheriff McCloud could speak to Darcy, but only about the newest death and only for twenty minutes.

Julia didn't like the parameters of the meeting. And, honestly, she hated that Darcy was the one calling all the shots, but as they prepared to leave, she said to Luis, "We owe Tom Dolan and his family to find out what happened. I don't think we have any choice but to play Darcy's game."

The Northern Wyoming Correctional Facility sat on a remote strip of land about an hour north of Pleasant Pines. In this part of the state, no trees grew, leaving the landscape barren. Julia sat behind the steering wheel, and to her, it looked like they'd driven to the moon.

NWCF housed a wide-range of inmates—some, like Darcy, were awaiting trial, but for a variety of reasons hadn't made or been given bail. Others had been convicted of crimes and the regional jail was deemed to be the most appropriate facility.

Aside from the jail, there wasn't another building for miles. The perimeter was surrounded by two sets of fences that were topped with razor wire. The building, a one-story square, was made of gray brick. A gravel driveway led across a flat expanse of land, connecting the single gate to the main road. Julia figured the desolate location had been chosen to easily spot anyone who might make a run for it.

On a single guard tower a lone guard stood sentinel and looked down at their approach.

It wouldn't be enough if Darcy ever escaped.

Julia pulled up to the gate. A call box sat on a post. There was a burst of static followed by a disembodied female voice. "Can I help you?"

"Sheriff Julia McCloud, here to meet with Darcy Owens."

With a rattle and a whir, the gates slid open. The gravel parking lot held only half a dozen cars and Julia chose a spot in the middle. The metal-and-glass front door reflected the late morning sky, almost seeming to sparkle with the light. Both Julia and Luis locked their sidearms in the glove box. Taking a gun into the jail was strictly prohibited. Walking through the front door with a gun meant one thing: the firearm would have to be surrendered.

"Let's go," said Luis, opening the door and jumping from the truck.

She noted that he winced as he took a step. "How's the ankle?"

"I'm tough. I'll live."

She smiled. "I thought you'd say as much."

A pair of cameras placed above the doors monitored their every movement. The front door clicked, the lock disengaging, as Julia and Luis approached.

The front door led to small holding cell. An African American woman with her hair pulled into a tight bun sat in a control room behind a thick sheet of glass. She wore the gray-and-black uniform of all NWCF officers and stood as Julia approached.

"I'm Emily," she said with a small smile. "It's nice to finally meet you, Sheriff McCloud."

"It's nice to meet you, Emily," she said. "This is Luis Martinez. He's consulting on the case."

Luis asked, "Is Darcy Owens available to be questioned?"

A metal door that led out of a holding area clicked. "There's a conference room around the corner. It's where most of the inmates meet with their lawyers and such. If that works for you, I'll have her brought from her cell."

They entered a corridor that was filled with the scents of grease and pine cleanser. A door to the left was open. It was the conference room.

A metal table was bolted to the floor and was surrounded by four chairs, two on each side. A loop was bolted into the table so handcuffs could be tethered to the surface.

Julia settled into one of the metal-backed chairs. The rungs imprinted on her skin and she leaned forward, not entirely sure how to get comfortable. Then again, this room wasn't meant for comfort—only function.

The door opened and Darcy Owens shuffled through. Bile rose in the back of Julia's throat. It'd been months since she'd seen the other woman, yet the change was remarkable. The last time, it had been in that bunker, hidden deep in the woods. Darcy had been wounded and ill. At the time, she wore filthy clothes and her pallor was gray. Now, she was clean. Clad in an orange jumpsuit and shower shoes, her hair was long and dark, with blond roots showing.

The differences were so remarkable that Julia could almost believe she had seen two separate women.

Darcy's hands were cuffed. A chain ran through the handcuffs to a bellyband around her waist. Her feet were also shackled and tethered to the thick, leather belt at her middle. In short, the killer wasn't going anywhere.

Clattering with each step, she approached the table and sat in a vacant chair.

Emily cuffed Darcy's arm chain to the metal loop, then gave the chain a hard tug. "Let me know if you need anything, Sheriff," she said before retreating from the room and closing the door.

Darcy lifted her eyes. Julia's stomach roiled as their gazes met.

"Sheriff?" she asked. "I thought you worked with Rocky Mountain Justice."

"So you remember me?" Julia asked.

"Sure, you were at the Pleasant Pines Inn after the cook's suicide."

"I was also in the bunker in the middle of the woods." Julia placed her injured hand on the table.

Darcy lifted one shoulder and let it drop. "I don't remember much from the woods."

"Do you remember killing my predecessor, Carl Haak? Or attacking me with an ax?"

"I think you're mistaken," said Darcy. Her voice was cold and flat.

Julia's pulse raced and her temper flared. She drew in a breath, but it did little to calm her nerves or rage.

Luis spoke up. "We're here to talk to you about another case."

"My attorney said someone else died. What happened?"

"A body was found at the park in Pleasant Pines."

Darcy blinked. "When?"

"Sunday morning," said Julia. "We just got the toxicology report. The victim had excessive amounts of alcohol in his system, and the same anti-nausea medication you used to give your victims."

"You can't be charging me," said Darcy. "I've been in jail for months. I'm not your killer—not that I'm admitting to killing anyone now."

"Half of a two-dollar bill was found with the victim, as well," said Luis. "Who else, besides you, would know that you left one of those with each of your victims?"

"They left a ripped two-dollar bill?" Darcy repeated. "Interesting."

"Who else knew about the torn money?" Julia had her own guess. "Robert Carpenter?"

"Don't bring him into this." The chains around Darcy's wrists rattled. "He's nobody."

"It doesn't sound like he's nobody to me." Luis leaned forward.

"We've been in your home," Julia continued, raising her voice to be heard over the clanking of chains. "We've seen your diary. We know Robert used to protect you, Darcy. Is he still protecting you?"

Darcy's expression grew taut with rage. Obviously, the idea that Julia or anyone else knew about her past—and her darkest secrets—unnerved her. She refused to answer.

Julia leaned toward her. "Come on, Darcy. You can tell me the truth. Did he know about the money?"

Darcy clasped her hands together to stop the trembling. Then, like a curtain being pulled closed, her expression went blank. "What money? I don't know anything about any money. And I especially don't know anyone who'd know that fact, even if I did." Darcy smirked.

The smile was a challenge and it told Julia everything she needed to know. Darcy knew the identity of Tom Dolan's killer. And she would never talk.

Yet, why would she have agreed to speak to Julia and Luis if she had nothing to say?

"What's the matter, Sheriff?" Darcy asked. "You

don't look fine. In fact, you look like crap. Do you need a doctor? I can help with that."

You don't look fine.

The walls of the conference room seemed to close in. Julia's face and feet went numb. She needed to get out of the room…to escape. If not, she'd retch on the floor. Moving to the door, she beat on the metal with the side of her fist. Sweat trickled down her brow, leaving her hair damp.

"Julia? You okay?" Luis was on his feet.

The door opened and Emily waited on the other side.

Pushing out of the room, she stalked down the short hallway to the control room. Another NWCF officer—this one a middle-aged man with a graying beard—sat inside the office.

"Everything okay, Sheriff?" he asked.

"Just open the damn door," she said.

He did as he was ordered without further comment.

The electronic lock clicked, and Julia turned the handle. She pushed past the holding cell. Outside, she took in deep, gulping breaths, desperate for air.

Luis placed his hand on her back. His touch was light. "What happened in there?"

Julia leaned on the truck. "To be completely honest," she said, "I don't know." Staring at the window, she saw her own face superimposed on the reflection of the endless plains. It was then that the memory flashed, like a sliver of glass from a broken mirror.

In the bunker, Julia had spoken to Darcy while

trying to negotiate a peaceful surrender. *You don't look fine. In fact, you look like crap. Do you need a doctor? I can help with that.*

Then today, Darcy had repeated those same words.

It had been a triggering event. Julia wasn't as strong as she thought…or hoped.

"In the bunker, I offered to help Darcy. Told her that she needed a doctor. Then today, she said exactly the same thing to me…in my own words. It just, I don't know, pushed me over the edge."

"It happens," said Luis.

Sure, it happened to other people—but not Julia.

Luis's phone began to ring. He checked the screen. "It's Katarina."

"Let's talk to her in the truck," she said, hoping that she could put the incident with Darcy behind her.

After unlocking the doors, both Julia and Luis slid inside the truck. He answered the call and turned on the phone's speaker function. "Katarina," he said. "I've got Julia with me."

"I just finished reviewing all of the video sent from the inn."

"I hope you have some good news," said Julia. "Because we are fresh out of leads."

"Sadly, I don't have news at all. The woman knew enough to keep her face down. We never caught her on camera."

Julia asked, "What about a car? Did you get a license plate when she left?"

"She and the victim walked away from the hotel and she never returned for a car, either."

"What about when she arrived?" It was Luis who asked the question.

"That's what's most troubling," said Katarina. "She never did arrive."

"What?" asked Julia, even though she'd heard Katarina perfectly.

"Just what I said. The woman is never on video arriving at the bar. The first time she appears is when she leaves the pub with Tom Dolan."

"She's not a magician. She didn't simply appear," said Luis. "Is she an employee of the hotel? Could she have been working in the pub or the kitchen?"

"I'm way ahead of you," said Katarina. "There isn't any employee now who matches the description of this woman."

"Can you do me another favor?" Julia asked, the wheels of her mind spinning "Can you search the video and see if you can find Robert Carpenter's car near the inn on Saturday night? I don't have any particulars, so you'll have to find those yourself, as well."

"I'll check with the DMV and then search all the license plates that were in the parking lot."

"Thanks for everything," said Luis. He ended the call. "Robert Carpenter? What's that all about?"

"From the beginning, we've had a short list of those who might be responsible for the crime. Bethany Edwards and Robert Carpenter."

"But the person who was with Tom Dolan on the night he died was a woman, not a man."

"Was it? We don't have any clear video of her face. We have to find Robert Carpenter," she said.

"Agreed. Are you going to send out an APB on him?"

Julia started the engine and put the gearshift into Drive. "As soon as I get back to Pleasant Pines, I'll have the entire state of Wyoming looking for that man."

And what would happen to Julia after she made the call?

She hadn't given much thought to the conversation she'd had with her mother on Sunday night. God, it seemed like a decade had passed, not just a few days. But now, the more she sat with the idea of life in Connecticut—boring but predictable—the more she liked it. Was now the time to leave Wyoming? Not give up, exactly—she refused to think of it as quitting—but regroup and make a new life plan?

Chapter 14

The NWCF was only a dot in the rearview mirror when Julia's cell phone began to ring. It was nestled in the console that held the controls to the lights, siren and public address system. She glanced at the screen. The call originated from a Wyoming area code, but she didn't recognize the number.

After pulling to the side of road, she answered the call. "Sheriff McCloud."

"Sheriff, my name is Anna Carpenter. I found your card wedged into the front door yesterday."

Holding out the phone, Julia activated the speaker function. She mouthed the words *Robert Carpenter's wife* to Luis.

"Mrs. Carpenter, yes. I left the card because I'm looking for your husband, Robert. Is he around?"

"Robert? No." Even over the phone, Julia could tell that the woman was distressed. "I was hoping you knew something about where he went. I haven't seen him for days."

"Days?" Julia repeated. "When did you see your husband last?"

"Saturday afternoon," she said, before her voice trailed off.

Julia could well imagine the reason for Anna Carpenter's hesitation. Despite the fact that her husband was gone, she was still loyal to him—at least to a degree. "I can help you find Robert, but you need to help me. Where was he going?"

There was a long pause. "He left to run some errands, but never came back. To be honest, I knew he was lying to me, even before he left."

"Lying about what?"

"About where he was going. What he was doing."

"Which was?"

"Sheriff, my husband hasn't been the same since that woman was arrested. Darcy Owens, that killer."

Julia looked up and met Luis's gaze. "Oh?"

"Robert has always been easily distracted. But when we saw that Darcy Owens had been arrested it was like something shifted in him completely. The man I knew was gone—I just don't know how else to put it. Do you understand what I'm saying?" She looked distraught.

Julia thought she might. Still, she didn't want to make assumptions. "How so?"

Anna continued, "All he talked about was the

Darcy Owens case. He read about it in the paper, watched the news to catch whatever he could—it became an obsession, I guess you might say."

"Do you have any idea where he might be now?" Julia asked.

"None. That's why I called you. I thought you might know something."

"I'm sorry that I don't, but I do want to talk to your husband. It's important." Julia paused.

"Me and the kids have been staying with my parents. I only stopped by today to see if my husband was around."

"He's missing?" Luis whispered. "What are the chances that he's another victim?"

Julia shushed Luis with a finger over lips. Then she asked, "Is there anything you can tell me that might help me find Robert?"

"This won't exactly help you know where to look," said Anna, "but a few weeks ago, I woke up in the middle of the night. Robert had come home after I'd gone to bed, but I could hear him in the living room. It was half-past two in the morning and he was having a grand old conversation with another woman."

Julia winced. Spending a lot of time away from home and work—especially if that time was at a hotel—could mean many things. None of them had to do with being obsessed with a serial killer. "I can imagine that'd be stressful to you, Mrs. Carpenter."

Luis mouthed a single word. *Affair?*

It was exactly what Julia thought. She shrugged.

"Stressful? Hell, I was furious. I stomped downstairs ready to yell at Robert and his friend and tell them both to get the hell out of my house. But I didn't."

"Why is that?"

"Because there was no other woman. It was just Robert alone, talking to himself and answering in a woman's voice. Now, *that* was stressful. I confronted him, but he told me I was mistaken. I wasn't, but I dropped it and went back upstairs. Then I stood at the top in the hallway and listened. After a minute, he started talking again. His voice. The woman's voice. It gave me chills, but that wasn't the worst part," said Anna. "When Robert spoke again, he had a name for the voice he was mimicking... It was Darcy Owens."

An APB had been sent to every law-enforcement officer in the state to be on the lookout for Robert E. Carpenter. His car had been located hours before, abandoned in a ditch on the outskirts of Pleasant Pines. The vehicle had been searched—nothing of importance had been found—and now sat in the impound lot.

Despite the fact that everyone was looking for Carpenter, he was still missing.

Luis had set up a meeting with Wyatt Thornton. Thornton had been briefed on Anna Carpenter's interview. As a former behavioral specialist with the Bureau, Wyatt now worked with Rocky Mountain Justice, creating profiles of their suspects. He had a long history with Darcy Owens—he'd been the lead agent on her case several years ago. He'd made a wrong call—and it had cost him his job. When she surfaced in Pleasant Pines, Wyatt teamed up with RMJ to finish the job he'd started. Now, using the evidence already gathered, and this latest briefing from Anna Carpenter, he'd been developing a possible etiology of Robert Carpenter's own drive as a killer. All three of them sat in Julia's office, and so far, Luis didn't like what was being said.

Wyatt said, "According to the FBI, there are four types of serial killer. There are those who are thrill seekers and those who are drawn to the control of the kill. One is the mission-oriented killer, like Darcy, who's on a mission to make the world a better place. Never mind that her brutal tactics, or in killing innocent men, she was accomplishing the opposite of her goal."

"But Darcy sees the men as a threat, because of what happened with her father, and that's why they have to die. Is that right?" asked Luis.

"More or less," said Wyatt.

The bit about Darcy was interesting, but she wasn't their target anymore. Luis asked, "What about Robert Carpenter?"

Wyatt sat back in his chair and folded his arms. "His motivations are a little murkier than Darcy's. From everything I've heard, he's a visionary killer—as in he has visions, auditory or visual, that instruct him to commit crimes. Most documented cases have a religious association. As in 'A demon told me to kill my neighbor.' But it's not always true. Also, there's usually a triggering event."

"So in the case of Robert Carpenter, it could be Darcy's arrest that started the visions," said Julia.

"Don't forget, he worked at the White Winds Resort," Luis reminded her. "For me, he's her accomplice, his alibi be damned."

"Either of those could definitely be a traumatic trigger," said Wyatt. "My sense is that Carpenter feels as if he has to save Darcy. Maybe he feels guilt for what happened to her with her father."

"You think that he's committing copycat murders to make it look like Bethany was involved?" Luis suggested. "That if he can cast doubt on Darcy's guilt, she'll go free?"

"It's more than possible," said Wyatt. "It's probable that those are his motivations. And maybe he's after revenge—that's why he's stalking Julia."

His words hung in the air, and Julia suppressed the need to shiver.

"I have something else I've been wondering," said Julia as she leaned forward at her desk. "Could the visions tell the person to change their looks? If Robert Carpenter is our killer, he dressed up to look like Darcy. Is that possible?"

"Sure. But it gets worse. Often, visionary killers start to think they're the being that has been speaking to them. Robert Carpenter might not simply be dressing up like Darcy Owens—he might actually be becoming her, as well." It was a lot for Luis to comprehend. "So, is this associated with his gender identity? Sexuality?"

"For a visionary killer, gender or sexuality don't matter. Darcy, and what she represents. That's what's important."

"That brings up something else." Everything Luis heard just brought up more questions. "How could someone with this level of psychosis function well enough to lead a normal life? Get married? Have kids? Hold a job?"

Wyatt shook his head. "Most serial killers are highly functional. How could they get close to their victims if they don't appear to be healthy, functioning people? With Carpenter, it's even more so. His psychosis has been latent, with the tendencies awakened by Darcy's reappearance in his life—most specifically her arrest."

"Plus, Anna told us that Robert always seemed a bit detached," Julia added. "Remember Liam and Holly found Darcy's old yearbook, and her diary. Robert was her only friend. He sheltered her from her father's abuse. Maybe he's always been her protector. Maybe he still is, in some way he imagines."

Luis wasn't convinced. "And now Darcy's, what? Telepathically messaging him from jail?"

"I have my doubts that something so mystical is even possible. But I'm sure Carpenter believes there's a kind of psychic connection. Think about it this way, by being Darcy's selection." Wyatt hooked air quotes around the word. "Carpenter can more than emulate her—a person he sees as having power. He can become her."

"That's not very reassuring," said Julia.

"No," said Wyatt, getting to his feet. "It's not. And here's what's worse. Darcy, as a killer, at least lived in the real world. If left unchecked, Carpenter will lose this tether to reality. If that happens, there's no telling what he might do next."

Luis cursed.

Wyatt continued, "I have some more research to do, unless you two need anything else."

"Go," said Julia. "You've been helpful."

After Wyatt left the office, Luis turned to Julia. "No leads to follow. No statements to take. Not even a report to review. I hate sitting around and waiting for something to happen." He gestured to Julia's desk. "What're you doing?"

"Like you said, there's nothing new for us to do. So I'm going to catch up on some paperwork. Sitting here is going to get boring. It's late. You can go. I'll call you if something comes up."

He checked the time. It was 7:30 p.m.

After a moment, he stood. "Come on. Let's get something to eat. Afterward, we'll check back in."

"Fine, I'll go but only because we skipped lunch and I'm starving."

They left the building. The sun had slipped below the mountain peaks, leaving the sky awash in pink and orange. Sally's was just down the block. It was one of the things he liked about Pleasant Pines. He was able to walk almost everywhere—completely the opposite of Denver.

They approached the little restaurant. From the front window, he could see that all the tables were full. "You know," said Julia, "I'm not really in the mood for a noisy room. I don't think I can stomach shaking hands tonight."

"You want someplace quiet? I know where to go." They walked two blocks off Main Street, where a house had been revamped into a restaurant called Two Brothers Chicago Pizzeria. With a red-and-white awning, a sign on the door proclaimed Best Pizza Ever.

Luis opened the door. The whole lower level of the house had been gutted to create the restaurant. Counter. Tables. Pizza oven in the back. Two men who actually were brothers stood behind the counter. "Hey, Luis," said one of them.

"Dan. Steve. I'd like you to meet a friend of mine, Julia McCloud."

"You the sheriff?" Steve asked.

"I am."

"Then you're a celebrity. Tonight, your dinner is on the house."

"You really don't have to do that—" Julia began.

"We insist. What'll it be? Cheese, pepperoni or sausage?" Dan asked.

Steve added, "Or pepperoni and sausage."

"Pepperoni it is," she said.

"Just give us a whole pizza and two beers," said Luis. He led Julia to a table in the corner and they sat.

Silverware rolled in paper napkins sat on the table. Julia twirled a set through her fingers and back again.

"You're quiet tonight."

She shrugged. "Just thinking."

"About the case? Or what happened with Darcy at the jail?"

"All of it, I guess. Plus, the future."

Now his interest was really piqued. "Oh?"

"I spoke to my mom on Sunday night. She said that the US attorney in Connecticut is looking for A-USAs."

Dan delivered beers in plastic cups. Luis didn't like the way the conversation was going, and he drained half of his beer in one swallow. "Assistant US attorneys. That's interesting, but how's that part of your future?"

"I've seen some things—not just with RMJ, but in Afghanistan, as well. Until now, I've been able to handle it, but the thing with Darcy…" Julia shrugged and sipped her drink. "I'm not able to shake what happened in that bunker."

Luis's pulse began to race. The beer sloshed around in his empty stomach, giving him an early hangover. "You can talk to someone," he said.

Folding her arms over her chest, Julia leaned back in the chair. "For months, I've done all kinds of therapies. Physical. Occupational. Talk. It might be time to admit the truth. Being attacked by Darcy has changed me."

"You'll find ways to cope." He'd been starving

only minutes before, now his appetite was gone. Was Julia really planning to leave Pleasant Pines?

"Luis," she sighed. "You're not listening to me. I am looking for ways to cope, and it's called making a change."

"You can't work for the US Attorney's office. You aren't a lawyer."

"I finished my first year of law school. I can do two more. There will be jobs after that, or I can work while I'm in school. I have some money that my grandmother left to me."

Steve brought over a square pan filled with thick pizza. "Best pizza in town. Our own recipe that we brought with us from Chicago."

"Looks great. Thanks." She gave a smile, but it was gone as quickly as it had appeared.

The food did look good and smelled better, yet Luis didn't have an appetite. He picked up a slice. Cheese slid back onto the pie. He ate, chewing slowly. "What are your plans?" he asked, trying to smile. "I know you have some."

Julia shrugged. "I was hired as the interim sheriff. My term only lasts a year. For now, I'll stay and keep working the case. Besides, Travis Cooper should be sheriff, not me. He put in the time with the department. I'll do what I can to make sure he finishes out my appointed term." She took a bite of pizza, nodding while she chewed. "This is really good, by the way." After washing down her pizza with a swallow of beer, she continued, "Besides, the school term already started. I'd have a lot to do to get enrolled for the spring semester—see if my grades and scores will transfer. I haven't looked into everything I need to do. Maybe reapply and retake any tests. I don't see being able to leave until the end of November."

So that was it? She could be gone by Thanksgiving. He couldn't let her leave, not without fighting for her to stay. "I don't want you to go," he said. "Jinxy would miss you."

"Jinxy?"

"And me. I want you here, with me."

Julia looked up from her meal, her gaze meeting his. "Oh?"

Had his tone betrayed him, communicating what he'd felt since forever, but never had the balls to say?

He should be the good guy. The one with restraint. But, damn it. He wanted Julia now. He wanted to kiss her, to lose himself inside of her.

Was it wrong to let go, especially if it was just for one night?

"I want you," he said. The truth was as simple and complicated as those three little words. And now that he'd said them, what would she do?

She stood.

Luis's pulse started to race. Damn it. It'd been the beer talking. How could he ever take his words back and make things right with Julia?

Holding out her hand, she said, "Let's get out of here."

Chapter 15

The street was dark, save for pools of light cast by streetlamps. The shops along Main Street were closed and only a few cars had parked along the curb. The tangy scent of pine filled the night air. Julia walked next to Martinez. Neither one of them spoke.

Despite the cool night, Julia began to sweat as her pulse hammered, echoing in her skull. Too soon, they stopped in front of the door that led to Luis's third-floor apartment. Luis got out the keys and fumbled with the lock.

She'd gone to his home dozens of times, and yet now, she was nervous—unsure of herself and her rash decision. Turning, she scanned the street, and something caught her eye. There had been movement across the street. Had a face been peering out from one of the upper windows? She took a step forward and peered at the building.

Nothing. But she had seen something. Or had she?

Still, she asked, "What's across the street?"

"Businesses on the bottom two floors. The top floor is an apartment, but it's been empty for as long as I've lived here."

Narrowing her eyes, she stared at the long line of windows.

Luis placed his hands on her shoulders. He massaged her tense shoulders and leaned close. His breath washed over her neck. "I want you," he said, his whispered words dancing across her skin.

Julia forgot about the building across the street. She turned to face Luis and placed her palms on his hard chest. Her heart began to race, reminding Julia that she was not simply surviving—she was very much alive. "Kiss me, Luis."

His mouth was on hers as they stepped deeper into the shadows. Julia gave a gasp of surprise and delight. Her lips parted and Luis began to explore and taste and conquer. Julia wanted to be overwhelmed and taken. She pressed her body to his. His arms and shoulders were strong.

His hands skimmed her breasts, and she sucked in a breath. Through the fabric of her shirt and bra, he found her nipples and rolled them between finger and thumb. A fire, long forgotten, sprang to life inside of Julia. The blaze consumed her. And she had no intention of taming the inferno.

"Luis…" she said between the kisses.

He rocked into her. He was hard, and she groaned with want and need too long ignored. Pressing her back into the brick wall, Luis worked his hand down the front of her pants. She was wet and only wanted his touch.

It was as if they didn't capture this moment and bend it to their will, then it would escape and elude them forever. He placed his thumb at the top of her sex. A charge shot through Julia, and she bucked against the newest sensation. He moved his touch in a small circle, and her pulse thrummed as she was carried away by a current that led to a sweetness of oblivion.

Julia's world broke apart. Luis's mouth on hers. Lips. Tongues. Teeth. The sky was nothing more than a curtain of black velvet. The cool night air caressed her skin.

Yet, there was more to the physicality of the moment. She was with Luis. He was her best friend and knew her better than she sometimes knew herself. Despite the fact that Julia had decided to be rash, it didn't mean she was without emotion.

Except she couldn't help but wonder how their relationship would change.

As her pulse slowed, he kissed her again. This time it was more chaste than passionate.

Luis said, "If we were that hot together here, I just wonder how much better it will be when we have a bed."

Could Julia imagine a future that included Luis as a lover, as well as a friend?

Looking up, she met his gaze. But there was something else that caught her attention. A pop of light shone from across the street. It was almost as if lightning had struck one of the deserted rooms… yet, she knew better.

Luis turned. "What the hell was that?"

"There was a flash—like from a picture being taken—on the third floor." Slowly, she searched every window.

"Like I said, that apartment has been vacant for months."

"It's not now," she said.

The silence was split in two with a sharp crack. Gunfire?

"That's a door," said Luis. "It came from behind the building."

He sprinted across the street. Julia followed, just a few steps behind. They ran to the end of the block and rounded the row of buildings. The shadow of a figure sprinted down the alleyway and disappeared into the gloom.

Luis cursed, his speed increasing. She pushed her legs to go faster, to try and keep up, but at the same moment that she noticed a wooden door, set several inches into the brick wall. It was held closed with a rusted padlock, yet the hinges were askew.

Julia skidded to a stop and examined the door. There was a thin seam between wood and jamb. She worked her fingers into the break and pulled. The door moved, opening just enough for her to slip inside.

A single set of stairs went up. The top of the staircase was pitch-black.

She went cold. It was just like the bunker in the woods.

"Get a hold of yourself, McCloud," she said. She took out her cell phone and activated the flashlight app.

She knew that if she didn't climb the stairs now, Julia would forever remain a victim of Darcy Owens.

Setting her foot on the step, she climbed to the next stair.

And then another. And another.

Soon, she realized that that staircase led to the third floor of the building. The steps ended at another door. This one was open, so she edged inside. Light from the streetlamp below streamed in through tall windows, and from where she stood, Julia had a perfect view of the apartment across the street.

Luis's apartment.

From her vantage point, she also saw a nylon camping chair that was set in front of the window. Cans and wrappers littered the ground. Someone had broken into this location, not for a free place to stay, but because it faced Luis's place. She shivered.

Her only hope was that Luis was able to catch whoever'd been stalking her.

While placing her phone back in her pocket, Julia stepped farther into the room. Beyond the chair and discarded food, there was also a laptop that was connected to a small printer. The far wall was papered with pictures. Pulling a photo from the wall, Julia sucked in a deep breath. The image was fuzzy, yet unmistakable. It was a picture of Julia, arms lifted, as she opened the curtains to Luis's bedroom. It had been taken this morning. And there were more than a dozen pictures, all of her, taken throughout today, that filled the wall.

Certainly, Julia had noted the flash of a camera coming from this window. Which meant her make-out session with Luis had been captured on film.

The thought made her skin crawl. Who was stalking her? And why?

Luis sprinted down the alleyway. He knew that Julia had stopped following, but he dared not slow his stride or he'd risk losing his target.

On the darkened streets, it was all but impossible to gather any recon. What did he know about the person he was chasing? Build was average. Hair color was indistinct. Race or eye color? Forget about it. In reality, Luis was following a shadow.

His lungs burned with each breath. His legs ached with each step. A cramp pulled at his side. He ignored all the discomfort. Ahead, the figure ran down a side street that led into a residential area.

Luis pushed his legs to go faster. Rounding the corner, he pulled to a stop. The street, lined on both sides with neat homes, was empty. Yards were filled with flowers and trees. Sandboxes and swings. Picnic tables and plastic wading pools.

Yet, he was alone.

The sound of footfalls echoing off the pavement

was gone, replaced by Martinez's racing pulse and ragged breaths. It was as if the person had vanished.

Luis didn't believe in magic—only good old-fashioned police work.

He walked to the end of the block, paying close attention to each door that he passed for signs of a forced entry.

There were none.

He reasoned that it would be difficult for the person to break in to a house without Luis noticing. After all, he was only seconds behind.

Which meant what?

Looking at the phone again, he placed a call.

She answered on the first ring.

"Tell me you got the guy," Julia said as she answered. "Was it Robert Carpenter?"

"Sorry," said Luis. "He disappeared. Hell, I didn't even get a good look at him."

"I'll send out a deputy to look for anything suspicious. You have to get back here and see what I found."

"Where is *here*?" he asked.

"The building across the street from your place on the third floor. Somebody broke in through the back door and has been watching us, at least since yesterday." She paused. "There's a laptop here. It might give us a clue as to who we're looking for."

"Sure thing," said Luis. "I'll be there in a minute."

"I'll be waiting." Julia hung up.

As he walked, Luis placed a call.

"Hello?"

"Sorry to bother you so late, Katarina," said Luis. "We have a situation and I need your expertise with a computer."

"Tell me about it?" she asked.

"The details I have are sketchy. It's a laptop and we're looking for something that connects to the owner. I can bring it to you after it gets dusted for fingerprints."

"Don't worry about that. I'll come to you."

"Meet me at the building across the street from my apartment? Third floor. Come around to the back."

"Which door?" she asked.

Having walked the entire time while speaking to Katarina, Luis made it back to the last place he'd seen Julia. A door had been pried off the hinges and hung askew, but a padlock was still in place, leaving a narrow gap to enter by.

"Trust me," said Luis. "You'll know it when you see it."

"I'm on my way," said Katarina.

"See you soon." Luis ended the call.

The space between door and jamb was far too small for Luis to walk through. He had to turn sideways and hold his breath to gain entry. A single set of narrow stairs led upward. They'd end on the third floor, Luis knew. He had a similar set of steps where he lived, only his were at the front of the building.

"Julia," he yelled. "You up there? It's me, Luis."

Sure, yelling into the darkness was not a stealthy

move. But Julia had been twitchy and easily upset of late, so it wouldn't do to sneak up on her.

"I'm here," she called back. "Come up. Check out what I found."

Luis ascended the stairs, his injured ankle throbbing with each step. He came into an apartment that was a mirror image of his own.

In the dim light, his eye was drawn to a far wall, covered in photographs. Or, more precisely, photographs of Julia. "What in the hell?"

"Hell is about right," said Julia. She was standing by the window, surrounded by soft light. Her golden hair fell loose around her shoulders and for a single moment, Luis recalled the scent of her skin, the feel of her as he held her in his arms, and she came in the darkness.

Turning away, he focused on the wall. There was a picture of Julia standing on the sidewalk, aviator sunglasses in hand. He pulled down the picture.

"What do you think happened? Somebody broke into this place and has been taking pictures of you for the past twenty-four hours?"

Julia pointed to a laptop and printer in the corner. "He must download them to the computer and then print them off himself, too."

Luis said, "Katarina's on her way. If anyone can get some information off the computer, it's her."

Julia nodded. "We need to get fingerprints, too. I'll call Deputy Cooper to dust the room."

Luis paused. Julia was silent—uncharacteristically so. "What aren't you telling me? What's wrong?"

"Look at all these pictures." She gestured to the wall. "This guy has been watching me all day. But it's more than that. He was watching me this evening. He was watching us." She paused. "On the street."

Sure, there were a lot of questions to be answered, but for Luis—personally, at least—Julia had just asked the most important question of all. How could he protect Julia? Especially since the killer seemed to be nothing more than a shadow.

Chapter 16

Peter Knowles spent the day writing about what had happened to Tom Dolan over the weekend. True, he didn't have the cooperation of the local sheriff, but that didn't mean there wasn't a story to print.

He jiggled the mouse of the laptop and checked the time—10:15 p.m. With a sigh, he powered down his computer, happy to have something to include in the midweek edition of the *Gazette*.

The outside door rattled, as if someone had put a key in the lock. Peter stood.

"Hello?" he called out. Certain it was a reporter working late, he continued, "I hope you have something for Wednesday's paper. Right now, we only have one story." He was old school and still thought of all editions being committed to paper. Correcting his mistake, he said, "Or to post."

Nothing.

He grabbed the jacket from the back of his chair. The door jiggled again, harder this time.

Peter froze, gooseflesh covering his arms. He kept a baseball bat under his desk, and he reached for it now. Bat in one hand, he entered the newsroom. It was empty. Whoever had been trying to get into the newsroom was unquestionably gone. He set the bat in the corner and returned to his office.

The number of emails had increased by one, which was nothing new. Yet, the reference line got his attention.

Made you look.

Had the person rattling the door also sent the email?

Several photos were embedded in the email. Peter blinked, refocused and looked again. Yep. His eyes hadn't been playing tricks on him. Someone had delivered a bunch of photographs. The story the pictures told was easy to follow. The sheriff, Julia McCloud, was busy with her friend, Luis…well, getting busy. And on an abandoned street, no less.

Certainly, the pictures were, umm, entertaining—tantalizing, really. The question was, why would someone feel they were newsworthy enough to photograph in the first place, let alone send to him in an email?

* * *

Julia had given several orders and they'd been followed within minutes. First, she'd called Travis Cooper, the deputy on duty, and asked him to bring a fingerprint kit and a set of spotlights. He'd done both. The dark apartment was now ablaze with light and the deputy was diligently swiping surfaces with a brush and fine, black powder, trying to find a set of fingerprints.

Katarina arrived only a few minutes after the deputy. Walking into the room, she spied the wall full of pictures and stopped short.

"Oh, my," she said. "That's upsetting."

"And then some," said Luis. Julia couldn't help but notice that his jaw was tense.

Katarina turned from the wall and gazed at Julia. A communications expert, the other woman was in her fifties and the unofficial den mother of Rocky Mountain Justice. Even though Julia was technically no longer part of the team, Kat still saw her as part of the RMJ family. "You said you found a computer?"

The deputy had the laptop open and was swirling fingerprint dust on the keyboard. "I'll be done in just a minute," he said.

"Did you find any physical evidence on the machine?" Luis asked.

"That's the weird thing," said the deputy with a shake of his head. "There aren't any prints on the computer. What's worse, there's not prints on the food wrappers or soda cans." All the debris had been lined up on the counter in the adjoining kitchen. Every piece was covered with black dust.

"Which means that whoever it is was careful about not being identified," said Luis.

"That's what I'd assume," said Travis.

"What about in the rest of the apartment?" Julia asked. "Have you found any complete fingerprints, or any other physical evidence? Hair? Fibers?"

"I've found loads of prints all over the place," he said.

With a sigh, Julia folded her arms. She knew it'd take a while to get answers, it was just that she didn't like the idea of waiting.

"The good news is, I'm done with this." He held out the computer. "You can try and get on to the hard drive."

Katarina accepted the laptop and took a seat in the camping chair. "I can tell you a few things," she said. "This is a new computer, as in purchased within the past few weeks…or maybe even days."

"What else?" asked Luis.

Katarina drew her eyebrows together and tapped on the keyboard. "Nobody has used this machine to sign on to any email address. There haven't been any texts sent or received, either."

"Which means that this user was cautious about leaving any trace—electronic or physical," said Luis.

"There's more that I can look into," said Katarina. "But not here. If we're lucky, I'll be able to find out where and when this computer was purchased. That could lead us to a credit card receipt or at least video footage from the store."

Julia nodded, but she really wasn't listening. Her gaze was drawn to the counter and the line of soda cans. "The person might've been careful with their fingerprints. In the end, they were sloppy."

"What do you mean?" Luis asked.

Julia lifted a can from the counter. "There might not be fingerprints on the can," she said. "But there's DNA inside."

Calls had been made and despite the late hour, Chloe Ryder was able to secure a lab in Laramie to run the DNA tests, provided that the cans and wrappers be delivered overnight. Travis Cooper had volunteered to serve as courier.

By the time all the soda cans had been tagged and bagged and were ready for transport, it was well past midnight. Julia's body was sore, yet through it all Luis had remained by her side.

"Ready to go?" he asked as she engaged the lock to her office.

"Sure," she said, walking down the main staircase. A night guard was on duty and opened the front door as they approached. True, Julia was ready to go home. But where? Back to Luis's apartment or to her own house?

In the end, she decided to go back to his place. It was closer—only a few blocks of walking, versus getting to her house, which would have also meant driving her truck. Besides, Julia didn't relish the idea of being alone while Robert Carpenter was still at large. They walked without speaking until the door to Luis's apartment was open.

Jinxy ran up to the couple, purring loudly.

"Did you miss me?" Julia asked, scooping the cat from the floor.

"She's hungry," said Luis, so he filled the cat's dish with food.

After brushing her cheek against Julia's, the cat jumped down and sauntered to the food dish. Luis dropped to the sofa and kicked off his shoes. He laid back, his feet hanging over the edge. After pulling a discarded blanket over his torso, he said, "This has been a long day."

Julia was tired, too. She dropped onto a cushion next to him. Still, she felt as if something needed to be said. "I did something last night and I need you to know."

"Oh?" Luis sat up.

"I called your sister, Francesca."

"Oh." His voice dropped an octave. "Why'd you do that?"

It was as if her mind had been filled with cotton, and she couldn't form a sentence. Placing her head on Luis's shoulder, she said, "It's simple. I want you to be happy. I probably shouldn't have interfered, but I wanted her to know that you're a good guy."

"What'd she say?"

"She told you to be safe."

"But she's not ready to forgive me."

Julia shook her head. "Not yet."

Luis placed his lips on her temple. "Thanks for trying for me."

Julia fought to keep her eyes open, but in the end she decided to let them close…just for a moment.

The next thing she knew, she was being cradled in strong arms and carried. It was Luis.

"Sorry," she said as he placed her on his bed. "I must've dozed off."

"We both did," he replied. "It's after two o'clock in the morning."

The curtains to the window that overlooked the street were open. Light stretched out onto the floor. After pulling the drapes closed, Luis stood in the shadow…dark and dangerous.

"I'll let you get back to sleep," he said. His words, deep and seductive, wound around Julia, finding their way to her heart.

She watched him retreat and recalled thc feeling of his lips on hers. And how she clung to his broad shoulders as she came in the darkness. Her inner muscles tightened at the memory.

But there had been more to those frantic moments beyond eroticism. She had felt something, an emotion—it was more than tenderness. She had been one with Luis—body, mind and soul.

"Stay," she said as his shadow reached the door. "I don't want to be alone."

"I shouldn't." Even though she could only see his form, she knew that he had turned to face her.

Rising from the bed, Julia padded softly across the floor. She wound her arms around Luis's neck and drew him to her. He resisted a bit, then leaned into her, pressing his chest into her breasts. She placed her mouth on his.

Running his fingers through her hair, he pulled her head back, leaving her throat exposed. He placed hot kisses down her neck, to her shoulder and lower still, to her breasts. A fire of passion sprang to life inside of Julia, threatening to consume her with the flames…leaving nothing but dust and ash.

He moved his hand to her torso, and she reached for his shirt. What she wanted—no, needed—was to feel Luis's skin next to hers.

She pulled his shirt over his head and moved her mouth to his abdomen. She traced the outline of his muscles with her tongue, tasting the salt of his skin. And then she kissed lower, stopping at the top of his waistband.

He was hard and strained against the fabric of his jeans. She unfastened the top button before pulling the fly free. Julia had no idea what would happen in the morning, much less in the weeks and months to come. But as long as she had this night, she'd make it one to remember.

Hooking her thumbs through the belt loops of his jeans, she pulled down his pants. After spitting into her palm, she took him with her hand. Her strokes were slow and methodical. After swirling her tongue over his head, she took him in her mouth, as well. Her hand and mouth worked in concert. Luis got harder in her grasp.

"Hold on," he said. He gripped her shoulders, his

fingers biting into her flesh. "I'm going to lose it completely."

She stopped her manipulations. "That's kind of the idea."

Luis pulled on her shoulders, urging her to her feet. "I don't want to lose control, not yet. Not until I've taken care of you."

He kicked off his jeans, then pulled Julia's shirt over her head. She worked on her pants and stripped down, leaving him naked and her wearing only her bra and panties.

"Come here," he said, leading her to the bed.

Luis sat on the edge and slid back until he was in the middle of the mattress.

She straddled Luis, riding his length through her underwear. She lingered as his head touched the sensitive spot at the top of her sex. It was a delicious torture to have him so close and to be so intimate, and yet not.

Pulling aside the crotch of her panties, he slid a finger inside of her. "God," he moaned. "You're wet and hot and tight."

"I want you inside of me," she said. "Take me now."

"Not yet," he said. "Lift your ass up here."

Julia did as he suggested and swung around, with her rear near his face. It left Luis's sex next to her mouth. She knew what he wanted—in fact, she wanted it, too. Julia slid her tongue up and down his length. While she tended to him with her mouth, he did the same. He suckled the top of her sex as he slipped two fingers inside of her.

Desire built within Julia. It was a great wave that grew and rose until it crested and crashed down. Julia gasped for breath as she cried out. Her entire body thrummed as she went limp. He rolled her onto her back and Julia sank into the mattress and the blankets.

"I'm not done with you yet." He sat up before opening the drawer of a nightstand. From there, he removed a single condom and rolled it down his length. "Are you ready?" he asked.

Julia nodded, drunk on sex.

Luis hovered above her. Pulling off her panties, he placed a leisurely kiss on her lips. He tasted of her pleasure. Situating himself, he entered her in one slow stroke. Julia gasped. She didn't think the pleasure would begin again. But it was there, just under the surface.

For the first time in a long while, she felt whole and normal.

It wasn't simply the sex. It was Luis. He'd given her a rare and wonderful gift. He'd brought Julia back to herself.

She cried out with an orgasm that she didn't expect. Trembling, she clung to Luis's sweat-soaked back. His thrusts became harder and faster. He let out a long and low growl, the noise almost savage, before falling into her arms.

She relaxed, knowing that finally, she was safe.

Chapter 17

Luis woke. His arm was stiff, and his neck was sore. He didn't care. He'd held Julia all night. And to be honest, he'd endure any pain if it meant he could spend one more night with her in his arms.

Then again, who was he kidding? He knew that women like Julia didn't end up with guys like him. Hell, what was he? A washed-up football player. A guy who'd barely graduated from community college. A cop who had been forced to leave his department. Someone who hadn't spoken to his sister in years.

Julia was a hero, with all sorts of awards and medals to prove it.

Maybe he should be thankful for the one night. At least he knew enough not to hope for more. As quietly and carefully as he could, Luis rose from the bed and moved down the hallway to the bathroom. He came back a minute later and Julia was propped up in bed.

The blankets were draped across her chest, the swell of her breasts peeking out from beneath the covers. Her blond hair fell around her shoulders. Her lips were red and slightly swollen from kissing.

God, she was sexy as hell.

"Morning," she said with a smile. A smile was a good sign.

Luis retrieved his jeans from the floor, then stepped into them and pulled them up. "Morning," he said.

"I guess we should go to Sally's for breakfast and see what kind of gossip we hear," said Julia.

We. He liked the sound of that.

Rising from the bed, she slipped into her underwear and a T-shirt. "Mind if I take a shower first?" she asked.

"I'm not sure," he joked while running a hand over his crew cut. "My hair takes forever to get right."

"Smart-ass," she said, sauntering from the room.

Luis watched her walk away. He heard the water start in the bathroom and immediately thought about joining Julia in the shower. Then again, she hadn't invited him to come along.

Jinxy came into the bedroom. Winding through his legs, the cat began to purr. "Ready for breakfast?"

It was a dumb question. The tabby was always ready for food. After filling the dish and setting it on the floor for Jinxy, Luis brewed a single cup of coffee. The shower quit running as he took his first sip.

Luis picked up his tablet computer from the table. There was a notification that the *Pleasant Pines Gazette* had published a new story. Tapping on the screen, he waited while the Wednesday edition loaded.

Tourist Found Dead—Cause Undetermined.

The front-page article was accompanied by a picture of Sean Reynolds, arms folded, standing in front of the gazebo.

Shaking his head, Luis had to admit that Peter Knowles had a flair for drama.

He read on:

> Saturday night was supposed to be a celebration of sorts. Tom Dolan, an architect from Atlanta, GA, was in Pleasant Pines for a mountain-biking trip. Having spent the day biking, Tom and his friends went to the pub at the Pleasant Pines Inn.
>
> Drinks flowed and Tom caught the eye of a blonde woman.
>
> "She seemed to like Tom," said Sean Reynolds, brother-in-law to Tom. "I was happy that he'd met someone because his ex-girlfriend had married some other dude."
>
> Arm in arm, Tom left the pub with the woman and that was the last time he was seen alive. His body was discovered in the gazebo at the town park the following morning. No of-

ficial cause of death has been released, leaving a grieving family with more questions than answers.

Luis set aside the tablet as Jinxy rushed past and jumped onto the windowsill. The cat stared into the street, the end of her tail twitching. She looked over her shoulder once, pinning Luis with her stare.

Luis approached.

Across the street, slumped against the building, was Sean Reynolds. Even from a distance, Luis could see the gray pallor of the skin, the sightless eyes, and he knew that the other man was dead.

Julia stood on the sidewalk as a deputy photographed Sean Reynolds. They'd closed Main Street and mapped out the scene. The operatives from RMJ had been called in. Everyone knew their job and they were doing it well. She was getting used to the procedures that accompanied finding a corpse, and she hated that fact.

"Anything?" she asked Luis as he approached.

"I walked the whole street—there wasn't much in the way of evidence." He held up several translucent bags. The word *evidence* was printed on them with red ink.

Then again, they all knew who they were looking for: Robert Carpenter. What Julia didn't know was how to find him.

Sawhorses had been set up at each end of the

block, yet a familiar figure approached. It was Peter Knowles.

"Man, that guy doesn't know when to give up," Luis growled. "Give me a second to get rid of him."

"Actually, you're right, he doesn't know when to give up and that's something we need." She maneuvered around the roadblock and met the editor halfway up the street. "You got a minute?"

"I was just about to ask you the same thing." He handed his phone to Julia. "Someone sent these to me last night."

A spiderweb of cracks filled the screen and her face warmed, realizing that she was the one who'd broken his phone. Yet there was more to see. There were four images—all of Julia and Luis. The pictures were explicit, despite the fact that not an inch of skin showed. And then, Julia's face flamed red and hot.

"Where'd you get these? Is that what you wanted to talk about? You need a comment to go with these pictures before you publish them?"

"Calm down and give me my cell back before you break it some more," he said, snatching the phone from her hand. "I'm not going to publish these pictures, but I wanted you to know that someone had taken them."

Julia exhaled, tamping down her anger. Sure, she was still mad as hell. It was just that Peter wasn't to blame. "There are some not-so-pleasant things that have been happening in Pleasant Pines and I'm hoping you can help me bring a very dangerous person into custody."

"I told you from the beginning, you can count on me."

"I'm hoping that I can." Julia glanced over her shoulder. Luis was directing the investigation. She motioned to him that she'd be back in five minutes. He gave her a thumbs-up and she turned to Peter. "Let's talk in your office. I'd like to get a look at the original email. Maybe we can learn something from the IP or the address."

"Sure thing," said Peter. "But you have to tell me what's going on."

Julia shoved her hands in the pockets of her coat as they walked. "First, there's been another murder."

"Another one," Peter said incredulously.

"Sadly. Sean Reynolds."

"Are you freaking kidding me?"

"I wish this was all some kind of sick joke." She paused. "I'll tell you everything, but give me your word that you'll help alert the public. Today. Now."

"You have my word." Peter stopped at the newspaper's office. "I have to ask you something else first. In looking in to your friend, Luis Martinez, I've come up with some interesting facts."

Julia narrowed her eyes and glared at the editor. "Which are?"

"I've been doing some digging. What do you know about a shadow agency called Rocky Mountain Justice?"

The cold air cut through Julia's uniform coat. She began to shiver and folded her arms across her chest. "No comment."

"Here's what I think. I think your friend Luis works for RMJ now and that you used to work for them, as well." He pointed to her injured hand. "And I think that Darcy Owens did that to you."

Julia fought to keep her expression neutral. "No comment. And I don't know how any of your conjectures matter. There's a killer on the loose. Do you want to inform the public or not?"

"Of course, but I also want to know what that agency is doing in my town."

"If you can help me find the killer, then we can talk. Deal?"

Peter opened the door. "Let's get started."

Pausing on the threshold, Julia said, "Have you ever met a man named Robert Carpenter?"

Peter shook his head. "Never."

"Get used to the name," said Julia, stepping into the office of the *Pleasant Pines Gazette*. "He's the guy we need to find before he kills again."

Sure, Peter had long ago decided to only publish two issues of the *PPG* a week. And, yeah, he had just released the Wednesday issue, but he also had the ability to send an article to readers directly, as well as post the story on the paper's site.

The headline: Town Holds Breath After Second Murder.

The article read:

> The body of a Caucasian male, name withheld until next of kin has been notified, has been

discovered in downtown Pleasant Pines. According to Sheriff Julia McCloud, "We see a strong connection between this death and that of Tom Dolan, which has been ruled as a homicide."

McCloud continued, "We also see a strong connection between these deaths and the murders committed by Darcy Owens."

Owens has been accused of committing over half a dozen murders in Wyoming and is awaiting trial at the Northern Wyoming Correctional Facility.

"At this time," McCloud concluded, "we have a single person of interest, Robert E. Carpenter of Slippery Rock, Wyoming. Carpenter is to be considered dangerous and should not be approached. If you see him, contact the sheriff's office immediately. Carpenter was last seen on Monday morning in Pleasant Pines."

Several photos of Robert Carpenter were attached to the story, including a photo of the blonde with Tom Nolan. That, law enforcement had surmised, was Robert Carpenter in a wig. According to his conversation with Julia, Carpenter was more than dressing like and emulating Darcy Owens. He saw himself as an extension of the killer. In fact, his personality was morphing to match hers. Along with the article, there were photos taken from the security camera at the Pleasant Pines Inn. Then, the entire file was uploaded.

With other stories Peter had written over his lifetime, he'd shared the facts and informed the public as to what had occurred. But this being was proactive. For the first time, Peter had the ability to stop another crime before it happened.

It meant that this article might be the most important that Peter had ever published.

Travis Cooper shifted in the seat of his cruiser and drew in a lungful of air. He'd driven all night to drop off the cans and wrappers at the state crime lab in Laramie. He'd been promised that the tests would be run first thing.

He was now on his way home, speeding down the interstate. Sunshine slanted over the mountains and the dashboard clock read 7:54 a.m. He wasn't going to lie, he hated working the overnight shift. His girlfriend, Cassidy, worked at the hospital during the day and Travis only saw her as he was coming home from work and she was leaving.

It was a lousy way to work a relationship.

What made matters worse was that Travis was still a deputy and not the actual sheriff. After years of dedication, he thought he deserved the position. Not that Julia did a bad job. She was smart, hardworking and driven.

Despite the long hours and the other hardships, Travis would never think of leaving the force. Being a cop was his calling. The need to protect and serve was embedded in his DNA.

And speaking of protecting, his eye was drawn to

the next exit. He could take it, making his trip home longer, yet he could also stop by Sergeant Taylor's house. Taking a drive-by now would save him from having to come out later.

Easing into the turning lane, Travis figured he could use a little fresh air, and he wanted to stretch his legs, too. Soon, he was turning onto the gravel lane that led to the Taylor home. The house was quiet and dark, just as it had been every other time he'd stopped by.

Putting his cruiser in Park, Travis turned off the engine and slipped out of the car. He stood, and blood rushed down his legs and filled his feet with pinpricks of pain. He stomped his boots, smothering any discomfort. As he had every other time he'd stopped by, Travis walked around the property.

Nothing had changed.

He strode onto the porch and glanced through a window. It was the same sitting room, filled with pictures. He tried the doorknob—it was locked, but…

The door wasn't latched.

The last time Travis had checked out the area, the door had been locked and closed.

Had the old man come home without Travis being told? Possibly. Yet, if he had, where was the dog?

Something wasn't right.

Unsnapping the latch on his sidearm, Travis pushed open the door.

"Mr. Taylor," he called out, stepping into the entryway. "It's Deputy Cooper—you home?"

He listened for an answer. None came.

Travis moved farther into the house. Past the stairs. Into the kitchen.

The counters were clean. Dishes filled a drying rack. A TV sat on the counter. Nothing appeared to be out of place, or even recently used.

Maybe Travis had been wrong about the door being completely closed all this time. Or maybe Sarge had stopped by yesterday and not locked up properly. Either way, the house was empty now. Travis retraced his steps.

He examined the door and the lock. There were no signs of damage or tampering. And yet, something had caught his eye. Travis looked at the small sitting room. On the back wall, there was a gun cabinet made of wood and glass.

Shards of glass littered the floor. One of the slots was empty. There was a creaking on the stairs and Travis slowly turned.

Christopher Booth, the leader of the Transgressors, a motorcycle club, stood on the steps. He aimed a shotgun at Travis.

"Deputy Cooper." He sneered. "I should've killed you last time. Oh well, problem solved."

And then, he pulled the trigger. There was a flash of light, a cloud of smoke and Travis was knocked into the back wall. His shoulder was filled with fire and blood soaked through his uniform and dripped onto the floor. Travis lifted his own gun and pulled the trigger. Booth ducked, but Travis continued to fire.

The Transgressor ran for the door and out into the woods.

Stumbling forward, Travis slammed the door and engaged the lock. His brow was soaked with sweat. His shirt was covered in blood. Leaning on the wall for support, Travis reholstered his gun and removed his cell phone. He placed the call.

"Julia," he said, as his vision started closing in from the sides. "He was here. Booth. He's got a gun."

Travis slipped down the wall. "I've been shot."

Then the phone slipped from his hand and clattered to the floor. A pool of blood spread out around Travis, seeping under his phone. As his vision went dark and his mind blank, he had a single and final thought. Had he even made the call at all?

Julia stood on the sidewalk. The body of Sean Reynolds had been transported to the morgue, yet the scene was still being processed for clues. With a phone pressed to her ear, her chest was tight. "Travis? Travis! Can you hear me?"

She knew he couldn't.

But she'd heard what he had to say. Christopher Booth had a gun. And, moreover, the bastard had shot her deputy. Yet, Travis had been cryptic in his location. *He's here.*

Sure, Julia could try and pull up Travis's location from his cell phone or use one the satellites RMJ could access to find his location. But that would waste time that she didn't have.

Then again, there was one place that made sense.

She began to jog down the street, toward her office and her car. "Luis," she called. "Come with me."

He drew his eyebrows together but ran to her side. “What’s going on?”

“I just got a call from Travis. From the little I got, he encountered Christopher Booth and was shot. See if you can find a signal for Travis’s phone.”

They stood in the parking lot behind the county office building. Julia unlocked the driver’s side door of her truck and slid into the seat. “Sure thing,” said Luis. “But where are you going?”

“My hunch is that Travis is at the Taylor residence. Call me once you find out about the phone, especially if I’m wrong. Also, send an ambulance.”

“Call you? I’m coming along.”

Honestly, Julia was tempted to keep Luis at her side. They hadn’t talked about their love-making last night, but certainly there was something to be said. And more than the physical turn their relationship had taken, she’d come to rely on him. He was beyond being a friend or a colleague—he was actually her partner.

Then again, the reason they hadn’t talked about their relationship was fairly simple. This was beyond the two of them. A murderer was on the loose in Pleasant Pines and it was up to Julia and the rest of the team to stop the killings. Someone had to stay and head up the investigation.

She shook her head. “We can get more done apart than together.” Sliding the key into the ignition, Julia continued. “We’ll keep in touch by phone. Find out where Travis called from. And send an ambulance to the Taylor residence, just in case." She turned the ignition and started the engine.

"Take care of yourself," said Luis as he slammed the door closed.

Julia shifted the truck into Reverse and pulled out of the spot. As she drove away, Julia glanced in her rearview mirror. Luis held the phone to his ear and placed a call. It would be to Emergency Services for the ambulance, she knew.

Lights on and siren blaring, Julia dropped her foot on the accelerator. "Hang on, Travis," she said to no one. "Help is on the way."

All she could do was hope that the help arrived in time to make a difference.

Chapter 18

The Watcher was in the woods, huddling at the base of the tree. Using an app on a stolen phone, they read the newest article posted on the *Pleasant Pines Gazette's* website. Stomach erupting, vomit splattered on the ground. Wiping a shaking hand across his mouth, Robert couldn't help but wonder…what next?

The whole world knew their name and what they'd done.

There was no taking it back at all.

A soft touch tickled Robert's neck, and he turned.

Darcy sat on the ground beside him. He expected a beatific smile, but her eyebrows were drawn together and her expression was as ominous as a thunderclap. "What have you done?" she asked.

"Everything you asked," said Robert, his voice shaking. "I did everything."

And he had—he'd tried to frame Darcy's cousin, a woman she hated. He'd tried to destroy the sheriff's reputation. He'd even tried to rid the world of those whom Darcy sought to smite.

"You tried," said Darcy, reading his mind. "But you failed."

"I did it all for you..."

"You know that you'll have to go away, don't you?"

He did. He nodded.

Darcy stroked the side of his face. "Kiss me, lover, before you're gone."

She placed her lips on his, just the lightest of touches. And then, the kiss became deeper, hungrier. His thoughts mingled with hers, until the lines between them disappeared and Darcy consumed Robert with her embrace.

And then, he was no more, and Darcy was reborn.

It was 10:32 a.m. Peter could have gone home. The good Lord knew he'd put in more than a month's worth of work in just a few short days. The fact was he wasn't tired—he was energized. And maybe he was holding out a little bit of hope that someone would call the office with a Robert Carpenter sighting.

That would make for a good headline.

And maybe a second Pulitzer Prize nomination...

The front door of the office opened and Peter leaned forward in his seat. "Hello?"

A woman, tall and blond with a scarf around her throat, appeared at the door to his office. "Good morning," she said. "Sorry to bother you. I'm looking for Peter Knowles."

"You are...?" asked Peter. The woman wore a lot of makeup.

"A concerned citizen," she said, her voice raspy.

He'd learned over the years to be suspicious of everyone and everything. Just to be safe, Peter reached for the baseball bat under his desk. Damn. He'd left it by the front door last night. "What's this regarding?"

"I saw your story this morning about Robert Carpenter. I think I know where he's hiding."

Placing his hands on his desk, Peter leaned forward. "You do? Where?"

"Are you him?" the woman asked. "Are you Peter Knowles?"

Like a fish on a line, Peter was hooked. "Yeah, that's me." He reached for a pad of paper and a pen so he could take notes. "Where is he?"

"Peter," said the woman. "You seem like a really good reporter. I'm surprised you haven't figured it out yet."

There was something in the woman's tone. A challenge. A taunt. A threat.

Peter looked closer at her.

The woman had a gun, with the barrel pointed at Peter's chest. She smiled.

He saw it then. The cosmetics were thick and expertly applied. But the scarf had slipped, exposing the throat and an Adam's apple.

"You?" Peter asked. "You're Robert Carpenter?"

Robert tsked. "I'm not Carpenter—he's gone."

"Where'd he go?" Peter's gaze was fixed on the gun.

The man's finger rested on the trigger guard. "It's almost like he never existed."

"But where…?" And then Peter knew. "You? You're Darcy."

"She's been locked up for too long and had to break free. It was the only way."

Peter's heart began to race, and his mind was filled with a swirling mess. It was impossible to come up with a decent thought, much less make a decision. Then a small voice whispered in his ear, giving Peter one piece of advice. *Keep him talking.*

"You don't need that gun," said Peter.

"Oh, don't I?" The man extended his arm, shoving the gun forward.

"You don't," Peter repeated. He lifted his palms to show that he wasn't a threat. "I know that you want to tell your story, otherwise you wouldn't have come to me."

Robert sneered. "That's where you're wrong. I never wanted anyone to know anything about me. I had the perfect plan that your most recent story ruined. Now you have to die."

"Killing me won't change anything that I've published," said Peter.

"You're right," he said. "It won't. This isn't about

fooling the police anymore. What I'm after is good old-fashioned revenge."

Peter had been around long enough to know crazy when he saw it. There was no talking to this man and if he wanted to survive, then he was going to have to fight. Rising to his feet, Peter hurled his laptop at Robert's face.

The other man lifted his arm to deflect the blow. Peter was already on the desk and he launched himself at Robert. In that moment, he recalled all those months he'd spent as an embedded reporter with the troops. How during a firefight, time slowed, and one second expanded until it filled hours and hours.

As he sailed through the air, time began to creep.

Robert stood erect. A *pop* filled the small office. A tendril of smoke wafted from the gun's barrel.

The pain was immediate and blinding with intensity. He toppled to the floor and gripped his shoulder before realizing that he'd been shot. Hot blood flowed through Peter's fingers and pain radiated through his body with each beat of his heart. As Robert Carpenter loomed over him, Peter knew that his story was about to end.

Without concern for the speed limit, Julia made it to Sergeant Taylor's house in record time. Skidding around the corner, Julia said a silent prayer. The EMS crew was already on site.

Parking on the lawn, Julia turned off the ignition and raced to the house. The door was open. She stopped short on the threshold.

Travis was lying on the floor, his skin a pasty white. The wall was painted red with blood. A team of EMS workers kneeled at his side and provided medical care. One was an African American man in his late twenties. The other was a gray-haired Caucasian woman of around fifty.

The male paramedic looked up as Julia entered the house. "We're trying to get the deputy stable enough for transport. Then we're meeting a medevac unit for transport to the hospital in Cheyenne."

Julia had been flown to the trauma center before, though she didn't recall a second of the flight. She nodded.

The EMT continued, "He's been given some meds for pain. It's going to make him groggy."

Travis was lifted onto a gurney. The legs were still collapsed, and sat flush with the floor. She kneeled next to Travis and his eyelids fluttered open. "It was Booth," he croaked. One shoulder was tightly bandaged, but with his other hand he pointed toward the sitting room. She immediately saw it—the gun cabinet with the shattered glass. "I think he broke into the house after Sarge left. He had a gun." He wheezed.

Julia placed her hand on his. "You save your strength for getting healthy. We'll find Booth." *And make him pay for what he's done.*

"Do me a favor. Tell Cassidy..." Travis's eyes drifted closed, the meds finally taking effect.

"You just get better and you can tell her yourself," said Julia, though she wasn't sure if he'd heard anything.

"Excuse me, ma'am," said the female. "We have to get the patient into the ambulance. The helicopter is on the way."

Julia stood, making certain that she wasn't in the way. "I'm coming with you."

The house needed to be searched and the woods had to be scoured for signs of Booth. But first, Julia needed to make sure her deputy was safely on the helicopter. Besides, she could make calls in her truck as easily as she could while standing on Sarge's lawn.

Following the ambulance, Julia placed her first call to Rose at the sheriff's office.

"I need an APB on Christopher Booth," she said as Rose answered the phone. "He was last seen at Sarge's house and it looks like he's armed. He shot Travis, who's in an ambulance, ready to be transported by air to Cheyenne."

"Another APB?" Rose echoed. "That's two in as many days."

"Whoever said that small-town life was boring has never lived in Pleasant Pines," said Julia.

"Consider it done. Anything else?"

"Text me with Cassidy's phone number. I need to call her and let her know what happened."

"Sure thing," said Rose, and then Julia ended the call.

Before Julia called Travis's girlfriend, she needed to get in touch with the rest of the crew. She was more than a little thankful for RMJ. Without them, her department would never be able to handle all of the open and active cases.

She placed the call, and Luis answered.

"Anything new on the search for Robert Carpenter?" she asked.

"Nothing. No reports of home invasions. Or stolen cars. If Robert is still in the area, he's found a hole to hide inside and isn't planning on coming out."

It was one of Julia's fears that they'd never find him…or bring him to justice. She recalled each time she'd encountered Robert over the past several days. He'd been more shadow than man. "I need some people to meet me at Sarge's house. According to Travis, Booth was in the home. He's armed and he's on the run."

"Which means he's dangerous."

"Exactly. I'm going back as soon as I make sure Travis gets his flight to the hospital."

The ambulance slowed and pulled into a large field. A helicopter, white with a red cross emblazoned on the side, hovered overhead.

"I'm here. We'll connect soon," she said, and ended the call.

As Julia put the truck in Park, the helicopter touched down. The transition from ambulance to aircraft was seamless and Julia wondered if it had been as easy for her. The medevac was airborne within seconds. As the downdraft kicked up dust, the male EMT gave Julia a smile and a wave.

She returned both.

The ambulance drove off and Julia remained. Without the roar of the helicopter's engine or the continual *thump, thump, thump* of the rotors, the field was absolutely silent. Julia glanced at her phone. Cassidy's number was in a text from Rose.

What had Luis said about calls like this? Oh, yeah—they were a gut punch. Well, he was right. He'd also said to be professional, honest and kind. Julia sucked in a deep breath and called the number.

"This is Cassidy."

"Hi, Cassidy, this is Julia. Uh, Sheriff McCloud. I have some news. It's Travis."

"Travis?" the other woman echoed.

"I'm sorry to tell you this. He was shot and is being air-lifted to Cheyenne."

"Shot? By who?"

Julia recalled what had happened—it was Cassidy's daughter who had been involved with Booth and ended up being forced into prostitution. It was Cassidy's insistence that had brought the Transgressor's illegal activities to light. "It was Booth. I'm sorry," Julia added, her throat sore.

Drawing in a ragged breath, Cassidy said, "I have to go. You said he's being taken to the hospital in Cheyenne?"

"I watched the helicopter take off myself."

"I'm leaving work now."

"We'll be in touch," said Julia.

She turned her truck around in the field and pulled back onto the road. She put on neither her lights nor the siren, but she did drop her foot on the accelerator. Seventy miles an hour. Eighty. Ninety. Ninety-five. She passed an oncoming car. It was just a whir of gray and silver, and her jaw tightened. Her heart began to race.

And then her mind recognized what her eyes had seen.

Dropping her foot on the brake, she fishtailed to a stop.

She looked in the rearview mirror. The rural road was empty and the car was gone.

Had she really seen Robert Carpenter, wearing a wig, pass her?

What were the odds?

Not good, she knew.

But would Julia ever forgive herself if she didn't turn around and at least check?

Peter Knowles's head slammed against something hard and he woke with a jolt. For a single second, he hung suspended between sleep and wakefulness, and decided that it all had been a horrible dream.

The stench of exhaust, the roar of the motor and the scorching pain in his shoulder told a very different tale. Peter had indeed been shot and then thrown in the trunk of a car. How long had he been out? He had no idea, and what's more, a part of him didn't care.

It could have been minutes…or maybe even days.

The car hit another rut, sending Peter up before slamming down.

Every part of his body ached, and his eyes began to drift closed. Sleep, he knew, would numb the pain.

No. He needed to think, to act, to survive. Slowly,

he moved his feet and hands. He hadn't been bound by ankle or wrist. His left arm moved, but his right arm was frozen—he figured that the bullet had shattered his shoulder.

Tenderly, he felt the wound. His touch was like a hot poker and he screamed as a great wave of agony pulled him under. Sweat covered his brow and lip. Yet, the pain helped him to think. Focusing on his breath, Peter reached into his coat pocket and found his phone.

There was no service—that would have been too much to hope for. But using the light, he could see his surroundings. Just like he suspected, he was in the trunk of a car. The emergency release handle had been cut away. He clawed at the nub…to no avail.

The car slowed and turned. It began to go up an incline. There was crunching under the tires. Gravel?

And then, the car stopped.

Adrenaline filled Peter's veins. What should he do? Fight? Feign unconsciousness?

The car door opened and then slammed with a thud that rocked the trunk.

Quickly, he activated the record feature on his phone and shoved it back into his pocket. Peter hadn't had a chance to form a plan. The trunk sprang open. The sunlight was blinding, and Peter shielded his face.

"I'm glad you aren't dead yet," said Robert. The other man still held his gun. "I didn't want to drag your body through the woods. Get up."

While covering the war, Peter had seen countless

brave men become submissive when facing an armed foe. At the time, he hadn't understood the change in demeanor. If one knows that they face death, why not die fighting? Yet, in this moment, he understood. It was the complete lack of power that had made the men malleable. Peter also knew that he couldn't refuse the order, even if he wanted.

At least he still had his cell and it was still recording. His only hope was that someday, somebody would find his phone. Only then would the final chapter of his life story be told.

The more Julia drove, the surer she became.

Her instincts had known.

The driver had been Robert Carpenter. But where in the hell had he gone?

She'd turned around on the road, but the car had disappeared. Then again, Julia knew he was out there…somewhere.

She had a hunch as to where Robert Carpenter might go. But was her intuition enough of a reason to check it out?

Her phone rang and she opened the call. It was Luis.

"Julia, where are you?" His voice was filled with static. She checked her coverage and only had one bar. "Liam and Marcus are at the Taylor residence and you aren't. Everything okay?"

She paused. Was she willing to share what she'd seen…or thought she saw? And really, should Julia be shirking her responsibilities? Sitting taller in the seat, she chose her direction. "I think I passed Robert Carpenter on the highway."

"What? Where? License plate? Make and model of the vehicle?"

"That's just it—I was going fast and just caught a glimpse. It was a sedan, I think. Gray or silver."

"That doesn't give us a lot to go on," he said, his words choppy as the coverage faded in and out.

"By the location and the direction he's heading, I know where he's going," said Julia. "He's heading home—that or to Darcy's old house. Either way, I have to check it out. Bring backup, just in case." She waited a beat. Then another. "Luis? Luis?" Glancing at her phone, she cursed. "Lost signal," she muttered.

But what had Luis heard? Would he know where to go? Or that she even needed backup at all?

Chapter 19

Luis gripped his phone and cursed. "Dropped call."

He stood on the sidewalk, at the exact spot where Sean Reynolds's body had been discovered earlier this morning. The corpse had been taken to the morgue, but Luis was still mapping out the scene. After Travis Cooper had been shot, the combined sheriff's department and RMJ teams had split in two.

As he'd told Julia on the phone, Marcus and Liam were looking for Christopher Booth, which left Wyatt and Luis in town.

"What's up?" Wyatt asked.

"Julia. She thought she'd passed Robert Carpenter. Her last words—before the damn call dropped—were 'By the location, and the direction he's heading, I know where he's going.'"

"I know one way to find out. C'mon. Let's head to RMJ and see if we can't find Julia on satellite."

The drive to RMJ was short, and soon, Luis and Wyatt were sitting in the computer lab. Wyatt programmed a satellite—on loan to RMJ from MI6, no less—to search for Julia's truck.

A grainy image filled the screen.

"That's Julia's truck, all right."

"Now," said Wyatt, his fingers dancing on the keyboard. "We have to figure out where she's going." The aspect expanded, until Julia's truck was just a flashing red dot on a picture of pixelated mountains, highways, ranches and homesteads.

Luis rose. "I know where she's headed," he said, halfway to the door. "Let's go."

Wyatt disconnected the RMJ server from the satellite. "Where to?"

"The home of a killer."

To keep from being seen or heard, Julia pulled off the side of the road a quarter of a mile from the Carpenter residence. Keeping to the ditch, thankfully dry, that ran between the road and the woods, Julia crept toward the house.

The roof came into view and she dropped to her belly, crawling commando-style for the last hundred yards. The scar on her stomach burned, but she let the pain provide fuel for what she needed to do next.

Even with the house, Julia crawled up the berm and peered over the edge.

Robert Carpenter, dressed as a woman—complete

with a blond wig—had Peter Knowles at gunpoint. How the hell had the newspaper editor ended up as the killer's hostage?

Robert was forcing Peter to walk away from the house and toward the woods. The reporter's shoulder was covered in blood. He'd been shot—by Robert, no doubt.

Julia crouched in the brush. Sweat trickled from her hairline and dripped into her eyes. She wasn't about to let Robert disappear into the woods with Peter in tow.

Peter's shoulder throbbed. His feet were too heavy to lift. His face burned and his hands trembled with cold. Despite the fact that he wanted to lie down and never get up, he walked on.

The sparse lawn ended at a wall of trees. He knew that if he stepped into the woods, he'd never come out. But he didn't have the energy to either fight or flee.

"Why?" he asked, his steps faltering. "Why'd you kill those men?"

"You can ask them yourself in hell," Robert said.

"I've seen war, man. So don't think that you're going to scare me with your talk of eternal damnation."

Robert, his blond wig askew, shoved him with the gun. Peter stumbled, but didn't fall. "Why do you care?" he asked. "You're going to be dead, too."

The phone in Peter's pocket was heavy and he wondered how long it would record before running out of battery or space. It was longer than he had, certainly. If he only had a few minutes to live, he might as well make them count. "I just want to know why. It's all I've ever really wanted. I guess it's the reason I became a reporter." He paused. If Peter wanted to survive, he had to reach the person inside of the monster. "Is Robert in there? Can I talk to him?"

Robert's eyes flickered, as though he was struggling to surface. Peter could only hope.

"You think that I'm going to tell you all my twisted secrets? Whatcha hoping for? That we'll be besties when you finally croak? Dream on."

Peter had interviewed thousands of people in his lifetime and he knew one thing to be true. Folks always liked to talk about themselves.

"Robert? Is that you?" he said, and then continued. "I heard that you dated Darcy in high school. Was that true?"

"I loved her," said Robert. They stood in the shade of the trees. Just a few more paces and Peter would be in the woods and lost forever.

"What happened?"

"She lives right over there." Robert pointed with his gun hand. "About two miles through the woods. Her parents didn't want her around other kids, but I could sneak over to her house and see her. At first, we were just friends and then..."

"And then?" Peter coaxed.

Robert pushed Peter. "Keep walking."

Peter stayed rooted to the spot. "And then what?"

Robert said nothing.

Peter took small steps. "Did she not love you back?"

"She loved me. We dated. I knew what went on in her house and even told her that we should...you know."

"Run away?" Peter offered.

"No, dimwit. Kill her parents. It was my idea. Make her dad look like an accident and then mom like a suicide. I thought that once they were dead, then we'd be together."

"And that didn't happen?"

"No way. She started living with Larry Walker, a real loser. They moved to Las Vegas and then came back a few years ago. I was married by then, so we never spoke. Until..."

"Until when?"

"Damn, you are persistent."

White lights danced in Peter's vision and his hand was numb. Blood dripped from his fingertips and landed on the arid ground. The bullet wound must've reopened. He was losing blood again. How much longer could he stay conscious...or even alive?

"She called me from the bunker, I guess. She needed help and I helped her. And after she was arrested, I couldn't sleep. She started talking to me."

"Calling you from jail."

Robert tapped the barrel of the gun on his temple. "In here." He tapped his chest. "And here. We're connected, don't you see? I was the one who helped her get free of her father, but she came to me and wanted me to continue her work."

"What will you do next? Your plan's been ruined." Peter's tongue was thick, and his words were slurred. He was hallucinating, seeing things that weren't possible. Like an image of Julia McCloud running across the lawn.

"Sheriff?" A moment too late, he realized that he hadn't been confused. Moreover, he had just ruined his best chance at escaping.

Julia's plan was simple. She was going to sneak up on Robert Carpenter and take him down. Just as she launched herself from the ground, Peter Knowles focused on her. "Sheriff?" he said.

Robert turned an instant before she wrapped her arms around his middle. Stepping aside, he missed her tackle. She still hit his wrist, knocking the gun lose. Drawing back, she lunged again. This time, Julia hit him on the knee.

Crying in pain, Robert crumpled to the ground. The wig slipped from his head.

She scrambled to her feet and brought up the toe of her shoe, catching him on the jaw. His head snapped back as blood spewed from his mouth. Twisting in the dirt, he reached for his gun.

She knew it was time to leave. But there was too much open ground between Julia and her truck. She'd never make it without getting shot, especially since she was bringing the newspaper's editor along.

It left her one option…and she hated to take it.

Grabbing Peter by the collar, she pulled him into the woods.

Luis drove his SUV, while Wyatt sat in the passenger seat.

During the drive, the two operatives had consulted with the team from RMJ. A plan had been made and as far as Luis was concerned, it was awful. Luis and Wyatt were to approach the residence and see if Julia was conducting surveillance on the subject, Robert Carpenter.

Beyond that, they were ordered to stand down and wait for the rest of the team, which was on the way.

They approached their destination, and Luis slowed. Julia's truck was partly hidden in a ravine. He pulled to a stop. From where he sat, he could clearly see the truck's interior. It was empty.

"She's not in here," said Luis. "You think she's in the house?"

"I hope not," said Wyatt. "There's a car in the drive."

Which meant that if Julia was inside, then she was trapped with the killer.

"I'm not waiting around for intel or firepower," Luis said. "You can wait for the rest of them if you want."

"No way," said Wyatt. "Your fight is my fight."

"How do we play this, then?"

Wyatt said, "We circle around the property by staying in the trees and come in through the back. It worked for us last time, when we got Sophie from Darcy. No reason it won't work now."

It made sense to Luis and he nodded. They got out of the vehicle, and he pulled his firearm from the holster at his waist. Wyatt was also armed.

"Let's do this," said Luis.

Traversing the woods, they exited the trees at the

back of the property, then Luis pulled up short. The thin lawn had been chewed up by a scuffle. Drops of blood led into the forest.

Wyatt kneeled next to the footprints in the dirt. "There are three tracks. By the size and weight of the impressions, I'd say two men and one woman."

"Julia," said Luis.

"Probably. Someone is bleeding." Wyatt stood. "Where do these woods go?"

"They stretch out for a mile or two and end at Darcy's house."

"I'll go through the woods. You take the SUV and drive to the property," said Wyatt. "One way or another we'll find them."

Luis ran back to his vehicle, not bothering to conceal his movements. Gunning the engine, he rocketed from the ditch. His tires kicked up a rooster tail of dust. He called his boss, Marcus Jones. "We have a situation," he said.

"Go ahead."

The cellular service was spotty, at best. Yet, Luis drove and told Jones about the footprints and the blood. "I think we have all three of them in the woods and they're going to Darcy's old house."

"We're still a few minutes out. Stand down until we get there."

No way was Luis going to follow that order. He ended the call.

The driveway leading to Darcy's house came into

view and, since help still hadn't arrived, it meant one thing. He had to go in alone.

Julia ran through the woods. She dodged branches and jumped over fallen logs. Her stomach burned, and she knew that there'd be hell to pay later—that was if she survived. All the while, she held on to Peter Knowles. She knew she could get farther, go a little faster, without him. But he was still alive, and she refused to leave him behind.

Peter was nearly comatose from blood loss. Walking dead is what they would've called him in combat. Yet, as long as he drew breath, she'd keep fighting to keep him alive.

Pines. Aspens. Scrub. Lichen on rocks that jutted from the earth. Ahead, she saw a trunk, splintered by a bullet. She skidded to a stop. This was where she'd mistakenly shot at Luis. Julia looked around. She recognized the area and began to retrace her steps from yesterday. The woods ended and Julia saw Darcy's home just beyond the tree line.

The abandoned house was far from an ideal place to treat a wounded man. But she'd been inside. She knew there were at least sheets on the beds that could be used to staunch the bleeding. Maybe she'd get lucky and find a first-aid kit. A ten-year-old aspirin was still an aspirin, right? Limping up the crumbling steps, Julia kicked open the front door. Stepping into the musty room, she stopped.

Standing in the middle of the floor, with a gun in hand, was Robert Carpenter.

He said nothing, and just pulled the trigger.

Luis was familiar with the sound of gunfire. It wasn't as loud as most people thought—like an explosion that could be felt in the teeth. It was a small noise, but it has the potency to turn a man's bowels to liquid, leaving anyone with sense running the other way.

Luis knew that instinct wasn't cowardice. It was all about survival.

But those who chose to protect and serve had to overcome that instinct and run directly into harm's way.

So when Luis heard gunfire come from the old house, he sprinted across the yard, mindful that he would be an easy target. But he was more worried about Julia's fate than his own. On the porch, Luis dropped to a knee and looked in one of the grimy windows. The interior was barely visible. Then he realized he wasn't simply looking through years of dust, but also a haze of smoke.

The acrid stench of burning fabric filled his nose a second before he heard the first crackle of flames. Luis opened the door. Smoke leaked into the afternoon, rising to the sky.

A figure was lying facedown on the floor. It was Peter Knowles. His shoulder was shredded and covered with blood. The curtains near the window smoldered. Fire spread from a hole that had been burned through the fabric. Luis rushed into the room.

"Peter? Can you hear me?"

Nothing. His skin was the color of used paste. His lips were blue. Luis felt for a pulse. It was faint, but there.

"I'm going to get you out of here," he said, slipping his shoulder under Peter's abdomen. With the other man draped across his back, Luis rushed from the house.

He laid Peter in the tall grass. The man moaned. "Julia."

Luis went cold. "Where's Julia. What happened?"

Peter lifted a limp hand and pointed to the house. "There."

"She's in the house?"

Peter gripped Luis's wrist with a strength he didn't think a man so gravely wounded could possess. Placing Luis's hand on his chest, he said, "You have to keep it safe."

Luis had no idea what Peter meant. *Keep what safe?* He looked to the building. Orange and black flames were visible through the window. He had to get to Julia. "Julia's in the house?" Luis asked again. "I have to get her out."

"Take it," said Peter. The whites of his eyes were bright red. "Keep it."

It was then that Luis realized Peter was pressing his hand onto something in the jacket's pocket. He reached inside and found a cellular phone. The recording device was on. "You want me to have the phone?"

Peter's hand slipped away, and his eyes drifted closed.

"Help is coming," said Luis as he used the fireman's carry to get the reporter to the SUV. After setting Peter in the passenger seat, he pressed a roll of gauze to the shoulder wound. "You need to hold on for just a minute."

Luis sprinted toward the house. A tongue of fire licked at the doorway and heat slapped him from twenty paces away. It was the stuff of nightmares, yet he didn't have a choice. Ducking down, he rushed into the blaze.

Julia had messed up, and badly. When Robert had fired the gun and missed, she'd done two things at once: told Peter to get away and then charged at the other man. She'd managed to distract the killer long enough for Peter to hobble toward the door. She had no idea how far he'd gotten.

Because, at that same moment, Julia had bolted up the stairs.

She'd taken refuge in Darcy's old bedroom, hoping that he would come after her and knowing that a defensive position was her best option. Sure, she couldn't hit the broad side of a barn. But she only needed to fire enough bullets to keep Robert occupied and give Peter time to escape.

The thing was, Robert hadn't followed.

What was worse was that smoke wafted under the

closed door. The floor groaned and Julia could feel heat through the soles of her shoes.

She knew that Robert was still out there, somewhere. To leave the room was to risk getting shot. To stay was to perish in the blaze.

Without a miracle, she was dead.

"Julia!"

Luis?

"Julia? Where are you?"

"Luis," she screamed. "I'm here. Upstairs."

The door burst open. A haze of smoke filled the room.

Robert stood on the threshold. Julia's eyes watered as she lifted the gun and took aim.

Chuckling, Robert shook his head. Lipstick was smeared across his face, making it look like a scream. "Why do you even bother? I've seen you try to shoot. You can't."

Then she remembered Luis's instructions. Pulling her shoulder farther across her body, she aimed again. Wrapping her finger around the trigger, she pulled.

There was a pop. A flash of light. The smirk never left Robert's face, even as his brains painted the wall.

There were footfalls on the stairs and then Luis appeared at the doorway.

He stared at the dead body on the floor.

"What happened?"

She answered his question with one of her own. "Where's Peter?"

"I pulled him out of the fire. He's in my SUV."

"Is he alive?"

"He was when I left him," said Luis. "Wyatt's on foot in the woods and the rest of the team is coming." Luis looked at the corpse on the floor. "We should go. The fire's spreading downstairs. The safest way is through the window."

It was an eight-foot drop. Luis held Julia by the wrists, lowering her as far as he could before letting go. She landed on her feet. A jolt of pain shot through her middle, and for a moment, she saw only a flash of white.

Luis dropped to the ground with a curse. Standing, he hobbled to her side. "You okay?"

"Sure," she said. Then, after a moment, the discomfort lessened. "Yeah, I'm better."

"Let's go and check on Peter," said Luis.

They rounded the side of the house. Wyatt stood at the door to the SUV and provided first aid. Dust rose at the end of the driveway and she knew that the rest of the RMJ crew had arrived.

"How is he?" Luis asked Wyatt.

"He'll survive, especially if we get him airlifted to the hospital in Cheyenne."

The SUV pulled to a stop in front of the burning house. An ambulance was right behind. Paramedics rushed to Peter. One of them used a satellite phone and called for a medevac and a firetruck. Julia thought that they should just let the house burn.

Marcus jumped out of the driver's seat at the same moment that Liam exited from the passenger side.

"Did you find him? Robert Carpenter?"

Julia pointed toward the inferno. "Whatever is left of Robert is burning up in that house right now."

"That's not entirely true," said Luis. He held up a cell phone. "Peter gave this to me after I dragged him from the house. The record feature was on. Looks like there's hours of a recording."

"Let's hope that Peter got a confession out of Robert," said Wyatt. "It'd help tie up the case nicely."

Luis's phone rang. He stared at the screen. Flexing his jaw, he tucked it back into his pocket and stalked to his SUV.

Julia followed.

"You okay?" she asked. "Who was on the phone?"

"That call was from my sister."

"Why didn't you answer?"

He shrugged. "What if I'm not good enough?"

Julia reached for his hand, slipping her fingers between his. "You're a better person than anyone could want."

"You say that…"

"I know it." Julia knew she couldn't heal Luis's wound with a few words. Still, that wouldn't stop her from trying. "You're an easy person to love, Luis, trust me.

He pulled her closer and wrapped his arm around her waist. "Love, is it?"

"Yeah," she said. "I think from the beginning, maybe."

"Maybe for me, too."

"Yeah?"

"Yeah." And then he asked, "But what does that

mean for us? For you? You caught the killer. You can leave Pleasant Pines now and let Travis Cooper become sheriff."

"Deputy Cooper was hurt bad. It'll take him a while to heal—trust me, I know the drill. Besides, I owe Peter Knowles an interview. After that, I was thinking about sticking around a while, if that's okay with you."

"Of course. But really, you have to have a plan. You always do."

"We'll start with you taking me home," she said. "And see where we go from there."

Julia stood in the lobby of the bank on Halloween. It was filled with children in costume—along with their parents, many of whom wore costumes, as well. She had come over after work and still wore her uniform.

The line of tellers' windows was decorated with cardboard cutouts of smiling witches and vampires. Orange and black garland ran the length of the counter. Tissue paper bats and ghosts hung from the ceiling. In the background, the Monster Mash played.

Despite it all, she smiled.

And she knew why.

For the past week, Julia had been staying in Luis's apartment. In all that time, she hadn't had a single nightmare. In the mornings, she woke refreshed, whole and calm. It was as if sleeping in Luis's arms had the power to stop the nightly terrors.

Or maybe she just dropped into a stupor after the fabulous sex they'd had each night.

Either way, Julia wasn't about to complain.

A plastic jack-o'-lantern filled with candy dangled from her hand. Luis stood at Julia's side. He wore a flannel shirt and jeans. Reaching into the open top of the pumpkin, he withdrew a small candy bar.

"Nice turnout," he said. After removing the wrapper, he shoved the chocolate into his mouth and chewed.

Julia nodded. "It is."

It seemed as though all of Pleasant Pines had gotten involved in the festivities. Every business on Main Street was handing out treats. Sarge and Sally had turned the diner into a kid-friendly haunted house. Peter Knowles, still hospitalized in Cheyenne, had organized the newspaper staff to turn the newsroom into a theater. They were showing Halloween cartoons until 8:00 p.m. After that, there was a horror movie double-feature.

A little girl, with cat ears, tail and a purple tutu approached Julia. She held open a canvas sack.

"What do you say, Sophie?" her father prompted. It was Liam Alexander, one of the team members from RMJ. With him was Holly Jacobs, child psychologist, author and survivor of a Darcy Owens attack.

"Trick or treat," said Sophie.

Julia bent forward, lowering the bucket to the child's eye level. "See anything in there that you like?"

Sophie nodded. "Uh-huh."

"Go ahead, you can pick your favorite. In fact, take two."

"Two?" Sophie echoed, her eyes wide.

Julia winked and let Sophie look through the candy.

"How are you doing?" Holly asked of Julia.

Lifting one shoulder, she let it drop. "You know how it goes. Some days are good. Some days are bad. At least I'm having more good days now."

"Trust me, I know how hard it is to get over everything that happened." Holly stroked Sophie's head as the child plunked two lollipops in her bag. "For everyone."

"I guess we have a lot in common—surviving what we have." Julia paused. "It's a sisterhood of sorts."

"You're right, it is," said Holly. And then, "We should get coffee sometime. It might be nice to talk to someone who really knows."

"I'd like that." Julia smiled. The expression was beginning to come to her more easily. "Thanks." Turning her attention to Sophie, Julia asked, "Have you already been trick-or-treating on Main Street?"

"We have." Sophie reached into her bag and withdrew a pink toothbrush. "See what the dentist gave me? I love toothbrushes and this has sparkles."

"I love sparkly toothbrushes, too," said Luis. "Can I have that one?"

"Mr. Martinez," said Sophie with a giggle. "You have to go trick-or-treating and get your own."

"It looks like there's pumpkin decorating," said

Holly, pointing to a conference table filled with small pumpkins, paints, stickers and markers. "Want to go and try it out?"

"Oh boy, I do!" Sophie held Holly's hand and skipped across the lobby.

As soon as Holly and Sophie walked away, Liam swatted his friend on the arm. "Where's your costume, man?"

"Me? What about you?"

Opening the front of his coat, Liam revealed his outfit. "See?"

"A shirt that says This Is My Costume doesn't count."

Julia laughed. "I have to side with Luis on that one, but nice effort."

"Speaking of effort, have you heard anything about the Carpenter case?"

Julia nodded. "I just got the lab results back from the cans and wrappers found in the abandoned apartment. The DNA matches Robert Carpenter's. There were hair samples collected from the room at the Pleasant Pines Inn that match Carpenter, as well. Combined with his confession to Peter Knowles, the evidence is clear. Carpenter was the copycat killer."

"And what about Travis?"

"He's in the hospital for the next couple of weeks. Once he's out, there's rehab. But his girlfriend is a nurse, so I think she'll take good care of him."

"Christopher Booth is still at-large, but the rest of the Transgressors go on trial in a few weeks," Luis added.

Julia continued, finishing the story, "I don't know if Travis will be back at work full-time until after the holidays. Still, he's hoping to be well enough to testify at the trial."

"You know, Holly and I were talking about Thanksgiving this morning. It's coming up. You're both welcome to join us for dinner. We'll have turkey. Gravy. Football. All the works."

"Thanks for the invite, man. I appreciate it." Luis slid his arm around Julia's waist and pulled her close. Her heartbeat raced. Julia wondered if there would ever come a time when Luis's touch didn't excite her. She hoped not. "But we've already got plans that weekend."

"Great. What're you two doing?"

It was Julia who answered. "Luis's sister invited us to her house for dinner."

"Your sister?" Liam echoed.

"I haven't spoken to her in years. I have a baby niece I've never met."

"That's awesome. You should definitely go. Maybe you can come over for dessert on Friday night."

"Count on it," said Julia.

Then Liam went to Holly, Sophie, and pumpkin decorating. Luis inclined his head toward the trio. "They're a nice family."

"They are."

"I miss seeing my sister. I'm glad this is working out." He paused and pivoted so he faced Julia. "Thanks for opening the lines of communication."

"You're welcome." Pride and contentment warmed Julia's chest—along with a tinge of relief. Her call could've easily caused more problems than it solved. She continued, "Besides, what're friends for?"

"Friends? I hope that we're a lot more than just friends."

"We are." Scanning the crowded lobby, Julia wondered if now was the best time to have this conversation? Then again, why not? "You are my best friend, but you're more. You're my cheerleader." She paused. "Luis, you're my everything."

"Julia," he whispered, pulling her to him. "I love you. I've loved you from the beginning, I think."

She turned to face him. "Luis, I love you, too."

"Tell me that you'll stay with me. I don't care if we're in Wyoming. Or Connecticut. Or anywhere else."

"Just try and get rid of me." She gave a flirtatious smile. "I'm with you for the long haul. I promise."

He placed his lips on hers. For half an instant, Julia hesitated. The sheriff shouldn't be kissing someone in public. Then she threw caution to the wind and wrapped her arms around him, barely registering the cheers from the crowd in the room.

Yeah, she was in love with her best friend—and she wanted the world to know.

Epilogue

Darcy Owens sat in her jail cell and read a newspaper that was a week old. The story was simple but left her nauseous. Robert Carpenter had posed as a blonde woman in order to kill two men. According to the article, DNA evidence linked Robert to the other crimes, as well.

There had been a standoff in the woods between Carpenter and local law enforcement. In the end, he'd died.

Julia McCloud, the sheriff, was quoted, and she said, "An employee of the White Winds Resort has confessed that Robert Carpenter, while a desk manager, placed Darcy Owens on the payroll and hid the killer's identity. There are other connections between Carpenter and Owens. Both have been implicated in the death of Owens's parents more than a decade prior. Charges for those deaths will be added to the long list of crimes that Darcy's been accused of committing."

The *Pleasant Pines Gazette* praised its recovering editor as well as the quick-thinking Sheriff McCloud. The story ended with a quote from the district attorney, Chloe Ryder. "Justice may be blind, but she's not stupid. Darcy Owens will stand trial for all the murders she committed and I'm confident that we'll get a conviction. She'll spend the rest of her days in jail, just where she belongs."

Julia McCloud. Chloe Ryder. They were to blame for Darcy's downfall. But they hadn't done it alone. Despite the fact that the operatives from RMJ hadn't been mentioned, she knew that they were involved, as well.

The Darkness coiled around Darcy's heart and squeezed.

It was then that she recalled a poster on a classroom wall. It been a poem by Robert Frost, with a misty lake in the background. She didn't recall the other lines, but there was one that she'd read again and again about only being free if she was bold.

She was bold. She knew what to do.

Darcy rose to her feet and walked over to the door. "Guard," she called out. "Guard!"

A young African American woman peered through the small window set in the door. Her name was Emily. "What do you want?"

"I need to see Chloe Ryder."

"The district attorney?"

"She's the one."

"I can't go bothering the DA without a reason."

"You need a reason?" Darcy didn't wait for an answer. "I'm ready to confess."

The woman's complexion turned gray. "You what?"

"You heard me. I'm ready to confess."

"Hold on one minute. I'll be right back."

Darcy could wait more than a minute. It'd been years, and now everything was finally in place. It was time that they all were made to pay.

* * * * *

Look for Marcus and Chloe's story,
the next chapter in Jennifer D. Bokal's
Wyoming Nights miniseries.
Coming soon to Harlequin Romantic Suspense!

COMING NEXT MONTH FROM

HARLEQUIN

ROMANTIC SUSPENSE

Available May 11, 2021

#2135 COLTON 911: HIDDEN TARGET

Colton 911: Chicago • by Colleen Thompson

Racked with guilt over an old estrangement, lone-wolf craft brewer Jones Colton hires the beautiful hacker turned PI Allie Chandler to solve the murders of his father and uncle. As unexpected attraction flares to life between them, Allie's daring techniques lead to possible answers...but will they come at a deadly cost?

#2136 GUARDING COLTON'S CHILD

The Coltons of Grave Gulch • by Lara Lacombe

Single mother Desiree Colton, desperate to save her son from a kidnapper, turns to Dr. Stavros Makris for help. But can Stavros, who lost his own child years ago, overcome his pain and keep them safe?

#2137 HER UNLIKELY PROTECTOR

The Riley Code • by Regan Black

Police officer Aubrey Rawlins knows Leo Butler needs help finding his missing sister. But as the two of them get closer to the truth, it becomes clear that someone with a lot of influence is determined to keep the truth hidden. Can Leo and Aubrey protect each other while saving his sister? Or are all three of them in more danger than they can handle?

#2138 THE NEGOTIATOR

by Melinda Di Lorenzo

When his nephew is taken, Jacob will do anything to get him back, even if it means accidentally kidnapping retrieval expert Norah Loblaw. Now they're working together to get Desmond back—and trying to explain their quickly growing feelings along the way.

SPECIAL EXCERPT FROM

HARLEQUIN

ROMANTIC SUSPENSE

When his nephew is taken, Jacob will do anything to get him back, even if it means accidentally kidnapping retrieval expert Norah Loblaw. Now they're working together to get Desmond back—and trying to explain their quickly growing feelings along the way.

Read on for a sneak preview of
The Negotiator,
Melinda Di Lorenzo's next thrilling romantic suspense!

He thought she deserved the full truth.

And I can't give it to her here and now.

"It's a complicated situation," he stated, hearing how weak that sounded even as he said it.

"Like Lockley?" Norah replied.

"She's a different animal completely."

The voices started up again, and Norah at last relented.

"Okay, I believe you need my help, and I'm willing to hear you out," she said. "Let's go."

Jacob didn't let himself give in to the thick relief. There was genuinely no time now. He spun on his heel and led Norah back through the slightly rank parking lot. When they reached his car, though, she stopped again.

"What are we doing?" she asked as he reached for the door handle.

"I'd rather go over the details at my place. If you don't mind."

"You don't live here?" she asked, sounding confused.

"Here?" he echoed.

"I guess I just inferred…" She gave her head a small shake. "I'm guessing it's complicated? Again?"

He lifted his hat and scraped a hand over his hair. "You might say."

He gave the handle a tug, but Norah didn't move.

"Changing your mind?" he asked, his tone far lighter than his mind.

"No. But I need you to give me the keys," she said. "I want to drive. You can navigate."

"I thought you believed me."

"I believe you," she said mildly. "But that doesn't mean I come even close to trusting you."

Jacob nodded again, then held out the keys. As she took them, though, and he moved around to the passenger side, he realized that her words dug at him in a surprisingly forceful way. It wasn't that he didn't understand. He wouldn't have trusted himself, either, if the roles were reversed. Hell. It'd be a foolish move. It made perfect sense. But that didn't mean Jacob had to like it.